DRUG GANG VENGEANCE

First published worldwide by System Addict Publishing in 2018

This edition published worldwide by System Addict Publishing in 2018

NEIL WALKER

By the Same Author

Drug Gang

Drug Gang Takedown: Drug Gang Part III

NEIL WALKER

For Louise

NEIL WALKER

Thanks to everyone who read the first Drug Gang novel and spoke to me about it, either in person or through social media. Without your encouragement and desire to see the story continue, this book would not exist.

NEIL WALKER

CONTENTS

NEIL WALKER

"That which does not kill us makes us stronger."

Friedrich Nietzsche

NEIL WALKER

DRUG GANG VENGEANCE
Drug Gang Part II

NEIL WALKER

NEIL WALKER

Chapter One

The adrenaline of violence can be an intoxicating and irresistible high. This is especially the case when you come away from a confrontation unharmed and victorious.

They made their way hastily away from The Doom Room, reasonably confident they hadn't drawn any undue attention on the way out. It was only a matter of time before the extent of the chaos they had just caused would be fully noticed and realised.

Getting away clean and clear was the priority and they couldn't afford to pause or slow down until they were in the car, driving away from the area.

The car was parked in a nearby deserted alleyway and the four of them scurried up to the rear of the car, while Alan pulled out the keys from the pocket of his jeans.

He quickly opened up the boot and John made no delay in reaching inside. In the boot were three sports bags, two of them large and one of them very large. The very large one was empty and hanging open, while the other two were zipped closed.

John immediately unzipped one of them, knowing exactly what he was looking for. He pulled out a torch, a large bottle of water and a small hand towel.

He rested the towel and the bottle on the edge of the boot and switched on the torch. He shone it first on his own hands then on his three friends, quickly scanning for blood.

They all had blood on their hands, not least John himself. Plus Blair had a little on his face.

"Okay lads, bring your hands in."

The three of them reached their hands close to John, as if they were about to join hands for a huddle and a team talk. John put one of his hands in after opening the water bottle and used his other hand to quickly pour water all over their outstretched hands.

He then switched hands with the bottle and washed his other hand of blood. They quickly passed the hand towel around between them, wiping and drying their hands.

John then picked up the bottle of water again and, without warning, squirted a big splash of it into Blair's face.

"Thanks for that mate," he said sarcastically.

He had his eyes closed and his face was still dripping with water.

"No worries," John replied in his faux Australian accent.

His attempt at an Australian accent was bad, although not as bad as Blair and Peter's imitation of a Northern Ireland accent, which was somewhere between Father Ted and Brad Pitt in The Devil's Own.

John threw the towel to him to wipe his face, before swiftly continuing the post-action clean up.

"Anyone got dirty weapons?"

Blair and Peter shook their heads, while Alan pulled out a set of blood-soaked nunchucks from the inside pocket of his denim jacket.

They were the varnished wooden kind of nunchucks, with rope in between the sticks, rather than a chain; what John and Alan referred to as Game of Death nunchucks, rather than Enter the Dragon nunchucks.

"Are you sure you got enough blood on those?"

Alan laughed, holding them out so John could pour water over them.

"It's not my fault these guys bleed like little bitches," Alan joked back.

This prompted a giggle from all of them.

John poured water over the nunchucks and Blair handed Alan the towel to wipe them down. They wiped clean easily and soon looked like they had never been used. Not that this would matter if the police stopped them, given that nunchucks were still illegal in the UK.

Although they all knew that they couldn't allow the car to be searched by the police anyway. The bag full of weapons in the car boot had a number of illegal weapons in it - including guns, which were very illegal.

John unzipped the other large sports bag in the boot, which was the weapons bag.

"Okay, fire those bad boys in there," he said to Alan, gesturing with his head towards the bag.

Alan threw them in and John zipped the bag up, before pausing to double check with the other two.

"Did you two just go bare-knuckle in there?"

"Yeah," Blair and Peter replied, perfectly in sync.

"Okay, we can sort out weapons again as we need them. Let's empty our pockets into the big bag."

John then reached into the boot and pulled the very large sports bag right to the edge.

They all emptied their pockets of money and drugs, pouring them into the bag. While there was a large amount of stuff that they emptied from their pockets, it didn't look like much once it was in this vast sports bag.

The night had only just begun though.

"Right boys, let's make like shepherds and get the flock out of here," said John.

John saying this prompted smiles and instant movement from the other three.

It was time to go.

They got into the car, Alan in the driver's seat, Blair and Peter in the back, John in the passenger seat; riding shotgun without a shotgun, or at least without a shotgun on him.

John looked into the wing mirror on his side as Alan started the car and they drove away. He realised he had forgotten to check if there was blood on his face.

Upon a close inspection, he found that his face was surprisingly blood-free.

He continued to stare at himself, however, as they quickly escaped the area in their car and started on their way to the next location; the next target.

Within a couple of hours it would be 2003, the new year that was supposed to signal a new life for John. He was aiming to be out of the game and embarking on a life of love, freedom and a kind of upbeat normality.

Exactly two months previously he had been sitting on his balcony in Australia, staring out at the water, reflecting on his happiness and thinking he had it all figured out. Halloween weekend in Sydney had been supposed to be a big one in terms of the drug business and from then until the end of the year had been all set to be a downhill ride.

The end of 2002 was meant to be the cut off for his drug business in Sydney and his life as a drug dealer.

Being a drug dealer was not how he had wanted to live his life. He had just viewed it as a means to an end. And a couple of months ago in Sydney, the end was just in sight…or so he had thought.

John had a carefully constructed plan when he was in Australia and he had intended to stick to it; so much for best laid plans. A lot can happen in two months and it most definitely had.

Now he had a new plan and he could still be out of the drug world by the time this night was over. There was a hell of a lot to do before then though and he would have to get a hell of a lot more blood on his hands.

Chapter Two

John was struck by the stark serenity of the jet black water, under the dark night sky, gently lapping endlessly beneath him.

He loved his balcony, his apartment, his view, and most aspects of his life in Sydney. Australia had been good to him since his return.

Circular Quay by night was peaceful and John found it soothing to just stare at it. He did a lot of his best thinking at night on his balcony, just looking out at the night view before him.

As he sat there, he reflected on how far he'd come in what was only really about eight months.

A year ago he had been in deep with Manchester drug gang The Brotherhood. He still had the tattoo on his arm, as well as some disturbing memories to remind of this time in his life.

The Brotherhood had been an incredibly violent, but extremely effective drug gang. Indeed, it was through the use of brutality without limits, striking fear into the hearts of their rivals, that they managed be so successful and almost unstoppable.

Ultimately, the drug business is not about drugs. It doesn't matter who has the best drugs. The drug business is about violence.

Which drug gang controls a particular piece of territory is dictated by which drug gang can insist upon itself through the threat of and the use of extreme force.

Despite the definitive action he had taken eight months ago, he still had mixed feelings about the whole Brotherhood period of his life.

Sometimes he would feel guilty about the terrible, violent acts he had been a part of, particularly what they had done to his good friend Michael and to Michael's mother.

Other times he would feel guilty about his own betrayal of the gang at the end. About killing Doug and Sanjay and robbing them to fund his escape and set up the life he was currently enjoying.

They had done terrible things, but so had he.

Forward was the way he had to look though. He had to force himself. After all, where does backwards reflection get you?

He had a business to run and a future to plan. The door to a way out and a happy, free, normal life was opening before him more and more. Love, life and adventure, rather than drugs, guns and violence.

It was all behind him in his apartment. His past, his present and what he hoped would be his future. Love in the bedroom, drugs, guns and money expertly hidden in the kitchen.

His own gang had grown from just himself, Peter and Blair, to a much larger operation. Peter and Blair had proved both loyal and capable and were now acting as lieutenants, dealing with the other gang members and getting a larger cut of the proceeds for themselves.

They had made a real impact in Sydney, thanks in no small part to lessons John had learned as a member of The Brotherhood in Manchester.

Like it or not, that gang had played a big part in making him who he was - in the drug world anyway.

Doug had told him he was just like him, right before John had shot him twice in the head. He may have had a point.

John decided to close up the balcony and go inside. Time for one last thought before he did.

Only two more months. Two more months of this violent, dangerous world and then he'd be out. He had calculated it carefully, before destroying the paperwork, of course.

All he had to do was stay alive and out of jail for two more months.

NEIL WALKER

Chapter Three

John quietly closed the balcony door behind him, as he made his way back inside the apartment. He then crept carefully through the main living area in his bare feet, hoping he could avoid waking Lisa.

She had been asleep for a while and had to work in the morning. More importantly, John had a few things to do that he didn't want her walking in on.

He walked as quietly as he could to the bedroom door and slowly pushed it open, just enough that he could see in without disturbing his sleeping girlfriend.

"Hey, what time is it?"

Lisa sounded half asleep, but was clearly not all the way asleep.

"It's three in the morning."

"Why are you still up?"

"I'm Night Guy," joked John.

This was his standard response.

"Day Guy is going to be mad at you," Lisa joked back. Her eyes were still closed.

John made his way into the bedroom and round to her side of the bed, careful not to let too much light into the room. He then sat himself on the edge of the bed, so that he was looking down on her face.

"I thought you were asleep," John whispered softly in her ear.

"Yeah, I think I was."

"Well why don't you just relax and go back to sleep. You've got work tomorrow and that shop isn't going to run itself."

Lisa laughed softly, her eyes still closed.

John began gently stroking her face from the edge of her eyebrow to her ear. Lisa smiled sleepily, knowing what he was doing.

This method was always guaranteed to put her to sleep, especially when she was already almost there.

It didn't take long for Lisa to drift off back to sleep and John quietly made his way back out of the bedroom, very gently closing the door behind him.

Things with Lisa and him were great. They had known each other and had a kind of on again, off again relationship in Belfast in their late teens. They had kept in touch via email since John went away travelling the first time and once she had mentioned a few months previously that she was coming to Australia, things between them had quickly got back on track.

As soon as she landed in Sydney, it was like they had never been apart.

They had a kind of shorthand like best friends, but with the romantic aspect added in. And as much as John enjoyed experiencing other cultures and mixing with people from other countries, spending time with someone who is from the same place as you, gets all your references without explanation and understands you in general was just so much easier and more relaxed.

It did mean leading a kind of double life, however. John had not told her about his current drug dealing exploits or his time in Manchester drug gang The Brotherhood.

How could he? Where would he begin?

Besides, even though she had tried her fair share of drugs and been on the periphery of the drugs world in Belfast, John was sure she wouldn't approve.

So he lied. He lied about his money and his recent past in the hope of keeping Lisa in his life and securing a great future for them.

She was the one, as far as he was concerned, and if all went to plan over the next couple of months, he would never have to lie to her again and she would never have to think less of him.

As far as she knew, he worked in nightclub promotions, which fitted perfectly with the lifestyle running a drug gang necessitated. He would be out at all hours of the night, in and around various nightclubs and tended to be very difficult to contact.

The fact that she worked a kind of nine to five job in a shop helped the whole thing run smoothly as well. When he was working at night, she needed to be sleeping and then when they did see each other, they would make the most of their time together.

John made his way into the kitchen area. He pressed the play button on the small stereo in the kitchen, ensuring that the volume was at a reasonably low, safe level before the music actually came out of the speakers.

It was a portable boombox with a single CD player and a single cassette deck, as well as a radio and two small built-in speakers. When John hit play, the CD player came to life, making the low hissing sound it always did as the CD started spinning.

Then the album 'Tellin' Stories' by The Charlatans began playing at a volume low enough to cover the noise of what John was about to do, or at the very least mask it if Lisa were to wake up before he had finished, but at the same time not loud enough to actually wake her on its own.

While it was not the most recent Charlatans album, it was still the 'new' Charlatans album in John's view, with anything they had done since being sub-par in his opinion.

With his cover music up and running and Lisa safely put back to sleep, it was time to begin the familiar routine of getting supplies organised for the weekend.

Even once he had the stuff out of its hiding place, there was still plenty to do when he met up with Blair and Peter. However, this was the tricky bit, in John's mind anyway; the risky bit when it came to his relationship with Lisa, which was the primary thing he cared about at this point in time.

He opened the third drawer down in the kitchen unit, to reveal a seemingly random and jumbled drawer full of mixed bric-a-brac and a few tools.

John reached to the back of the drawer and picked out an old and haggard looking wallpaper and paint stripping tool. John wasn't sure of the exact name for the thing, his education in the ways of tools and painting and decorating having come from his grandfather, who referred to this particular kind of device as a 'scraper'.

Scraper in hand, John knelt down on the tiled kitchen floor and opened up the cupboard under the sink. He then set the scraper down on the floor and began quickly and quietly taking out the assortment of cleaners and cleansers and carefully placing them on the floor behind him.

He was like a cat burglar during this process, wary of setting off an alarm - which in this case was any unnecessary noise that could wake his slumbering girlfriend.

If she caught him in this moment, it would be a tough situation to explain his way out of.

If she caught him at the next point, with everything exposed, he would be busted - caught red-handed.

He could not allow that to happen.

Chapter Four

With The Charlatans still playing through the kitchen stereo, John got down to the serious bit of the operation. It was time to delve into the hidden compartment where he kept the evidence of his secret existence. His other life in the world of drugs, guns and gangs.

With the door of the kitchen cupboard open wide and its contents all out sitting on the kitchen floor behind him, John went to work with his trusty scraper - and he did not generally use it for scraping off wallpaper or paint.

He wedged the sharp edge of the scraper under the bottom of the cupboard, forcing it into the small gap. Once it was firmly wedged in, he pushed it upwards - hard enough to raise it, but not so hard as to jar it and risk a bang.

When he had the bottom piece of the cupboard raised up far enough with the scraper, he took hold of it with his free hand.

He then set down the scraper and used both hands to carefully, and in a very controlled manner, lift out the large piece of veneered wood that made up the bottom of the cupboard. He placed it beside him on the kitchen floor and turned back to the cupboard.

At first glance, the now exposed area under the cupboard looked like concrete. This is how it was supposed to look to anyone else but John, anyone who was to ever get this far.

John picked up the scraper again and wedged it in between the vertical piece of wood at the bottom edge of the cupboard - which went right down to the tiled floor - and the apparent layer of concrete. He then pried up the piece of chipboard that he had painted to look like concrete.

Under here was his treasure chest. This was the hub of his illegal business, hidden discreetly under his kitchen sink - their kitchen sink.

The whole area was completely covered with a layer of carefully packed drugs, guns and money.

These had been placed there on a bed of coffee grounds and coffee beans. This was so that if his apartment was ever to be searched by police, not only would the officers be unlikely to find his carefully constructed stash area, but if they were to bring in sniffer dogs, they would literally be put off the scent.

He believed that the strong scent of coffee in a kitchen full of other strong, everyday smells would be enough to mask all of the illegal odours.

John quickly lifted out two large plastic bags of ecstasy pills, one large bag of cocaine and one large bag of base speed. He reasoned that this would be more than enough to cover them for what promised to be a very busy Halloween weekend, especially after they had jumped on the cocaine and the base.

Realistically, it would be a lot more than they would be likely to sell, even if they had an insanely good Halloween weekend. But John felt that it was best to be over-prepared and it would do no harm to have an extra supply of drugs for the weekends ahead that were 'nightclub ready'.

In Manchester, Doug and Sanjay would have cut the base speed into what was still very strong speed and cut the cocaine down by about fifty per cent. This was not The Brotherhood, however, and John's gang was not in England.

This was Australia and in Australia - particularly in busy, modern cities like Sydney - the demand for drugs far out-stripped the supply. The quality of the drugs available here was nowhere near that of the quality of drugs available in England, or in Northern Ireland for that matter.

In Australia they could really cut their powder down a lot and still be guaranteed to not only sell it, but also have happy customers coming back for more.

Cutting it was for tomorrow though; tonight was just about getting his supplies ready and packed up for meeting Blair and Peter the next day.

Finally, John reached in and pulled out a .45 automatic pistol. He slotted out the magazine to double check it was fully loaded, tapped the bottom of the magazine gently on the floor and then slotted it back into the gun.

He held the gun in his hand, paused and thought for a minute, then put it back into the compartment under the sink.

While he was generally a great believer in the philosophy that it was better to have a gun and not need it, than to need a gun and not have it, on this occasion he felt he could get through the Halloween weekend without having to pull or use a gun - or so he hoped.

Having placed the pistol back in its position in the hidden compartment - embedded among the coffee grounds and coffee beans - he carefully picked up the piece of chipboard painted to look like concrete and placed it back on top of the compartment.

Once he was satisfied that it was firmly in place, he picked up the veneered piece of wood that made up the bottom of the cupboard and wedged it firmly back in position. Then he quickly but carefully got the cleaners and cleansers back in the cupboard, in something resembling their original set-up.

Closing the cupboard door, John put the scraper back in the drawer, got up with the four bags of drugs cradled in his arms and carried them across to the table in the living room area.

One of the drawbacks of an open plan apartment like this was that he was still only one door and one surprise door opening away from being caught in the act and having some pretty tricky explaining to do.

Having placed the bags of drugs on to the table, he quickly made his way over to the small, hard leather, box style magazine holder beside the sofa and pulled out his sports backpack from within it. He then quietly hurried back to the table, opening his bag and removing the contents.

In the bag were a few bits of gym clothing and a zip-up leather wash bag. He unzipped the leather wash bag, took out the minimal contents - a small deodorant and some shower gel - and began cramming the four bags of drugs into it, being careful not to burst either of the bags of powder.

Once the drugs were safely zipped up in the wash bag - which was now absolutely full to capacity - he placed it at the bottom of his sports backpack. On top of it he then placed the deodorant and shower gel, followed by the gym clothes.

He then grabbed a colourful beach towel from the radiator and his red cotton boxing wraps from the plastic clothes horse, on which they had been hung to dry.

Red cotton boxing wraps were more traditionally associated with Thai boxing, with white cotton wraps being used in western boxing. Even though John was more of an enthusiastic and skilled practitioner of western boxing than any other martial art, he always stuck with the red cotton wraps, as he had studied Thai boxing first and had got used to them.

John was generally a very loyal person - even when it came to things like boxing wraps.

He threw the red boxing wraps and the beach towel into the sports bag, on top of all the other items and zipped it up; job done.

He placed the sports bag on the floor at the side of the kitchen table, beside the chair where he usually sat to eat breakfast. This served both to remind him to bring it with him in the morning and to ensure that he was the only one likely to have any dealings with it, when they were both getting ready in the morning.

With the stress of having to sneakily do his preparation for the next day without waking Lisa now at an end, he sat down on the sofa and took a deep breath. Time to unwind before joining Lisa in bed.

Tomorrow was going to be a big day. There were drugs to be cut and packed, training to be done and arrangements to be made for the full and busy weekend of drug dealing ahead.

Chapter Five

As Lisa rolled up the old metal shutters, the early morning sunlight cracked through the window, illuminating the souvenir shop.

It was a much less prestigious job than she had been used to in Belfast, but it was not at all taxing and she really enjoyed it. Lisa was a people person and there was no shortage of people from all over the world passing through this Sydney souvenir shop on a daily basis.

As she turned the key in the lock of the glass front door, the shrill alarm started to sound. She left the key in the door and she rushed into the shop to type in the alarm code before the alarm sound went from ear torture to ear piercing.

John stood in the doorway, holding the door open with his shoulder, while also keeping his fingers in his ears to drown out the torturous din. Lisa mercifully entered the alarm code successfully on her first attempt, before the alarm was allowed to drift into overdrive.

"Come on in and bring the keys," instructed Lisa.

She made her way towards the shop counter.

"No probs," agreed John.

He pulled out the keys and wedged the door open in the standard way.

This routine had become second nature for both of them. John then made his way through the shop and sat up on the counter top, facing his girlfriend.

"See, I told you we'd be on time," he said smugly.

"Yeah yeah, I could have done without the rush thank you very much."

"Come on, you know it's up to me to put a bit of excitement into your life."

Lisa looked up at John, smiling disapprovingly. She then put her attention back on the till, which she was setting up for the day.

While they had made it to the shop in time to open up, she was left with virtually no time to get organised before the daily parade of customers would start drifting in and out.

"Okay, well I've got things to see and people to do," said John.

He hopped off the counter on to the same side as Lisa and put his hands around her waist for a goodbye kiss.

"Give me some sugar," was his tongue in cheek kiss request.

Lisa obliged this request and they kissed, before John hopped back over the counter.

"I'll see you later tonight?"

"Hopefully, if you're still up when I get in," he replied.

He blew her a kiss over his shoulder as he made his way out of the shop. Lisa smiled and went back to her till preparations.

After only a few minutes the first customer came in. Lisa had got things set up for the day's work just in time.

As the guy made his way slowly around the shop - occasionally picking up a key ring or a fridge magnet for closer inspection - Lisa noticed he was wearing a Middlesbrough Football Club football shirt.

Lisa was by no means a football enthusiast, or 'soccer fan' as she'd become used to it being referred to during her time in Australia. She did, however, have an in-built radar for all things related to Middlesbrough Football Club, as John had been a big Boro fan the whole time she had known him.

This was very unusual in Belfast and indeed in Australia. It seemed to her - even with her limited knowledge of and interest in football - that most people in Northern Ireland and Australia seemed to favour and support the likes of Manchester United or Liverpool.

NEIL WALKER

So, just as it did with John, anyone wearing a Middlesbrough football shirt would always catch Lisa's attention. She would of course feel compelled to discuss the guy's football shirt choice with him, if he ever made it up to the counter.

As the guy approached the counter, she could see he was roughly the same age as her and John - approximately twenty-four or twenty-five. She prided herself on being good at guessing people's ages, although it was hard to get a really good look at this guy due to the fact that he was wearing a baseball cap.

When he got to the counter, he placed his selection down for Lisa to take payment and bag it up in the little paper souvenir bags the shop used.

After a few minutes of browsing, he had picked out a Swiss Army knife embossed with a Sydney motif.

Lisa didn't even pick it up before she launched into chatting mode. She knew John would want to know all the details about this random Middlesbrough fan.

"I see you're a Boro fan."

The guy laughed, taking off his cap and placing it on the counter beside the Swiss Army knife.

"Yep, for my sins," he retorted jokingly.

"My boyfriend supports the Boro, so I'm kind of obliged to say I do too."

"Really? That's unbelievable; two more Boro fans in Sydney. You don't sound like you're from Middlesbrough though."

"No, I'm from Belfast. We both are actually."

"Belfast? How the hell do you end up supporting Middlesbrough if you're from Belfast?"

Lisa laughed.

"Yeah, John gets that a lot."

"John?"

"Yep, that's my boyfriend's name."

"No way!"

"Way," Lisa responded.

She was unsure why he found this small piece of name trivia so hard to believe.

"Fucking hell. The only other Boro fan from Northern Ireland I've ever met was called John. It's probably just a coincidence though. I know it's a big place and you don't all know each other," he joked.

"Why, what was this guy's surname?"

"Em...I think it was Kennedy. Yes, definitely Kennedy."

"No way!"

"Way," he smiled back at her.

"That's my boyfriend's name. What age was he?"

"About the same age as me. I'd say twenty-three or twenty-four."

"My boyfriend is twenty-four. How crazy will that be if you know John?"

"Totally mental."

"Did you used to live in Belfast?"

"No. The John Kennedy I knew lived in Manchester at the same time as me."

"Oh my god, my John Kennedy used to live in Manchester. When was this?"

"I knew him last year and I think he was still in Manchester at the start of this year. I'm pretty sure we spent New Year's Eve 2001 together."

"Holy shit! Well there's no way this can all be a coincidence. My boyfriend John lived in Manchester at that exact same time."

"This is insane! It really is a small world. John is a really good friend of mine. We've been through a lot together."

"All good I hope?"

"Oh of course. All's well that end's well," he said, grinning and leaning his elbows down on the counter.

"This is great. He'll be so surprised and pleased to see you."

"I know. I really can't wait."

"Sorry, first things last; my name is Lisa. And you?"

"My name is Simon."

Chapter Six

John walked into the main area of the gym, having already got changed. He was carrying a weights belt and weights gloves, as well as boxing gloves, boxing headgear and the red boxing wraps for his hands.

The weights belt, weights gloves, boxing gloves and boxing headgear he generally stored in his locker at the gym, only very occasionally taking his weights gloves home to wash them. The red boxing wraps for his hands he took home to wash after every session, along with whichever towel he had brought with him

It didn't take long for him to locate Blair and Peter, who were already lingering round the heavy bag, laying claim to it.

They had started wrapping their hands and had a bit of a sweat going, having obviously done some light exercise to warm up. John would just stretch and join in with them, rather than going through the day's workout one step behind the pair.

They were focused on wrapping their hands and didn't notice John approaching. He gave them a shout out as he came upon them, heralding his arrival.

"Morning muthafuckaaas!"

Blair and Peter looked up in unison and smiled.

"G'day sweetheart, the girls' gym is up the road," Blair responded with quick wit.

This earned him a mild slap around the back of the head from John as he joined his friends.

"Have you been here long?"

"Nah mate, just about ten minutes. All you missed was a quick warm up on the rowing machine," Blair informed him.

Blair was doing all the talking, as was usually the case with him and Peter. He was more loud and brash, while Peter kept his head down and his mouth shut most of the time - although when he did talk, people listened.

Blair was a little younger than Peter and John as well, so having just turned twenty, he was still full of the enthusiasm and dynamism of youth.

"You gonna warm up?" asked Blair.

He was already nearly finished wrapping his hands and eager to get under way.

"No mate, I'll just stretch while you two go first. One minute rounds?"

"Sounds good," said Blair, while Peter nodded his agreement.

Peter had been a little slower in getting his hands wrapped, so Blair was clearly up first. Blair picked up the stopwatch from the ground beside them, set it for a one minute countdown, hit the button to begin timing his boxing minute and dropped it back down to the ground.

John looked on as Blair energetically threw skilled punches into the heavy bag, varying his angle of attack well and incorporating some shadowboxing technique into his bag work, just as John had shown him only a few months previously.

Blair absorbed everything John taught him like a sponge, both in terms of boxing and combat training as well as with regard to the drug world. He was somewhere between John's protégé and his adopted little brother.

Peter, on the other hand, was more like John's chief lieutenant. He and John were the same age and had been in the Sydney drug operation together from the start.

They had come a long way in just a few months, thanks to intelligent planning and the appropriate use of necessary violence. In Sydney, as in Manchester, violence was both the universally understood language and necessary evil of the drug scene.

Peter's skill set in terms of martial arts had been closer to the standard John was at when they started, in comparison to Blair. And he had improved to an even higher level with John's help.

Peter was well trained up in karate and had some boxing experience. John had vastly improved his boxing skill and knowledge and helped him focus on the aspects of his karate most useful in street combat. He had even taught him a few devastating Thai boxing techniques; the kind that tend to finish arguments.

Blair had started out as a boxing purist, but John had gradually encouraged him to incorporate techniques from Thai boxing and even judo. He had been reluctant at first, but as he saw how well the stuff he was learning worked in real world fighting situations, he took it on board more and more and was hungry to keep learning.

With a beep from the stopwatch, Blair stepped away from the heavy bag. He now had a full-blown sweat going and was quite out of breath.

Peter was up next and, after resetting the stopwatch, he began leathering punches into the bag, while John quickly got his hands wrapped. He would have preferred a longer period of stretching, but he wanted to be ready for his round.

This was a pretty standard part of their daily routine. They would meet in the gym in the morning - when it was relatively quiet - warm up and start off on the heavy bag. One minute rounds were a popular opener.

They would take turns to do a minute on the heavy bag and then would have a two minute rest period while the other two did their rounds. They would do this rotation a few times until they had a good sweat going and were fully warmed up.

Doing work on the punch bag with their hands wrapped, but not wearing boxing gloves, was another aspect John had brought to Peter and Blair's training. The reason for this was that - for their purposes - it was best to train as much as possible without gloves.

The point of their training was to be lethal with their bare hands in potentially deadly situations and speed and accuracy could mean the difference between life and death.

Training with boxing gloves on was essential for sparring, but for work on the heavy bag or with target pads, having your hands wrapped but without gloves had one distinct advantage. You were training yourself to be accurate with a fist that was literally the size of your fist.

Too much training with gloves on meant training yourself to be accurate with a fist the size of your head, which was fine for boxing in a ring, but not for fighting in the street or a nightclub.

John got his hands wrapped just in time for the next beep from the stopwatch, signalling his round on the heavy bag.

The training session would go on for the next couple of hours, before it was time to get John's sports backpack full of drugs out of the gym locker, take it back to Peter's place and begin cutting and prepping the drugs for the weekend's dealing.

NEIL WALKER

Chapter Seven

Peter lived by himself in a decent-sized, relatively normal looking suburban house. What was going on inside it was far from normal and suburban, however. It was time to get organised.

Peter's house had become the default location for cutting and packaging, as John lived with Lisa and Blair still lived with his parents.

It was not that Blair couldn't afford his own place with the money they were making; he was just lazy when it came to things like that. 'If it ain't broke, don't fix it' was his mantra.

Peter was happy to have them over and use his place as a kind of narcotics staging area. They were careful and low key, never drawing any unnecessary attention.

Besides, when it was at his place it meant that he got to pick the music. This is particularly important when you are sitting together for hours with music playing in the background, cutting and packing drugs.

Both Peter and John had similar musical taste for the world away from the club scene, but Blair's brain bounced to a techno beat. While techno music was great for clubbing, as far as Peter and John were concerned, it had no place in day to day living - even if day to day living involved preparation for clubs, drugs and violence.

The selection on the kitchen CD player as they got underway was the 'Odyssey #5' album by Powderfinger. This was an album that John and Peter both loved.

It had been the biggest album in Australia when John had been there before and had kind of soundtracked his travels around the country. While it hadn't necessarily been massive worldwide, John certainly felt it was one of the best new albums he had heard in years.

He smiled and nodded his approval as the opening chords of 'Waiting for the Sun' rang out in the kitchen, getting the usual warm and fuzzy feeling of nostalgia that he got every time he heard it.

"Good choice that man," he announced.

"Why thank you sir."

"Yeah, I suppose it'll do," Blair begrudgingly admitted.

When it came to this particular album, he was no different to the rest of Australia; he loved it. Not that he would admit this to the other two and he would certainly fight the urge to sing along to some of the almost irresistibly catchy choruses.

Everything was already laid out on the table. It was a sea of powder, pills, mirrors, razor blades, credit cards, little plastic bags and cling film.

They sat down across from each other at the round kitchen table to get started, setting up their own individual workstations with the materials at hand. The three of them were spread out evenly around the table facing each other, like three points on a triangle inside the circle of the table.

"Does anyone know where to get any coke?" Blair joked.

They all laughed and got under way.

John had never really been involved in this part of the operation when he was in The Brotherhood in Manchester. Doug and Sanjay had done all the cutting and packing, with Simon occasionally lending a hand.

If Sanjay had been Doug's chief lieutenant, then Simon had been his number one son.

By this point, John had become completely used to this aspect of the drug process, after months of regular practice. Peter had been the expert on this part of the job at the outset of their Sydney drug gang, having done it plenty of times before.

Prior to John arriving in Sydney, Peter had done some drug dealing and run his own small crew. He had been no stranger to cutting and packing drugs and he had taught John well.

He had also showed John just how much they could cut the cocaine and speed down by and still be deemed to be selling a good and desirable product. They cut their powdered drugs a lot more than The Brotherhood used to, but still had Aussie customers gladly coming back for more.

It was perfect.

After about twenty minutes of focussed cutting, with no one talking, Blair broke the silence.

"So, what are we going to do about The Hatchet Mob?"

This was a problem they were all aware of and which needed to be discussed.

"The Hatchet Mob," John repeated, sitting back in his chair and stalling for time a little.

Ultimately, he was in charge of this gang and he knew he needed to give the air of having everything under control and always knowing what to do. Uncertainty at the top leads to uncertainty throughout, John reasoned.

This was a tricky situation and Blair was right to bring it up. They had to know what they were going to do today, ahead of going out to work that night.

Both Blair and Peter had their own guys who reported to them, with John only dealing directly with these two. It meant less exposure and hassle for John and he trusted his two friends, despite them only having been in his life for a matter of months.

The reason that it was Blair who raised the issue - other than his inability to keep his mouth shut - was the fact that it was one of his guys who had been attacked the previous weekend.

The Hatchet Mob problem had the potential to get bigger before it got resolved.

John had put off dwelling on it during the week, as this was his time with Lisa and he tried to separate himself from the drug world and the issues within it, while he was spanning time with her.

He had been confident that when the time came he would know what to do. Now that time was at hand.

"How is Chris?" John asked.

He was genuinely concerned for Chris's welfare, but he also wanted to gain a few extra seconds thinking time.

"He'll live. I mean, he won't be dancing to 'Y.M.C.A.' any time soon, but he's getting better."

Chris had been beaten quite badly the previous Saturday night, with a marker being laid down for the weekend that was now upon them.

The Hatchet Mob was expanding their territory and the collection of nightclubs in which they controlled drug dealing. Their latest target was the notorious drug den nightclub Spice.

Spice had always been synonymous with drugs and indeed with violence. John's gang had been forced to fight hard to claim it among their drug club portfolio and he knew they couldn't afford to give it up.

This was not just because of the revenue generated from dealing in Spice, although this was substantial. It was also because if they blinked when intimidated by another gang - if they showed any weakness or hesitation - they would be in further trouble, with The Hatchet Mob and any other gang who heard about it. They had to make a stand.

"They won't get away with it; make sure Chris knows that," John reassured Blair.

"Do we hit them tonight?" asked Peter.

He fully understood the significance of their next move.

The Hatchet Mob needed no introduction.

Everyone in Australia had heard of The Hatchet Mob and the violent antics they got up to were the stuff of legend. Australians in general tend to love an outlaw and gang leader Hatchet Willis was practically a household name.

His nickname/street name and the name of his gang came from his tendency to use hatchets and other chopping devices. He and the rest of his gang used them to enforce their authority on the street and to strike terror and violence into their enemies.

There had been an infamous spree of people having fingers, and sometimes even whole hands, cut off and put in the mailboxes of family members about a year previously, which led to Hatchet Willis being incarcerated for a while.

After the case had been dismissed for lack of evidence, Hatchet Willis was back on the street and hell-bent on claiming and re-claiming as much territory as he could. He had been frustrated by his time locked up, but had come out feeling invincible.

John now had to show him that he was not invincible.

"Leave it to me," John confidently declared.

"What?" said Blair, taken aback.

"I'll take care of it. Just have a couple of your guys ready to move in and start selling when I text you it's done."

"On your own?" questioned Peter.

He was also surprised at John's bold declaration of intent.

"They think they can scare us and fuck with us. They need to be shown how wrong they are; how weak they are."

"Mate, I'd love to come down there with you and bring a couple of my guys. We could spread this lot out like marmite on a slice of toast," Blair interjected.

He was eager to be involved, but he was also concerned for John's welfare.

Blair knew just how capable John was and didn't doubt his prowess in a violent situation, but thought that perhaps he was underestimating the vicious intent and capabilities of The Hatchet Mob.

"Nah mate, I need the exercise," John joked.

"I've got a shotty hidden in the shed. Sawn off; nice and discreet," Peter offered.

"It's okay mate, I should be able to defuse the situation without anyone getting shot."

"They'll be tooled up to the teeth mate," Peter protested.

He was still keen for him to take the shotgun.

"True. I should probably bring a knife."

Both Blair and Peter really felt that he should have brought a gun or some manpower for back up, but Peter just got up from his seat and made his way to his kitchen cupboard.

He lifted out a box of cereal and pulled the plastic bag full of Cheerios out of the box. He then handed the box to John.

John tipped it upside down and smiled as a butterfly knife slid out of it into his hand.

"Nice; a butterfly knife. My favourite."

John was coming across as super confident and relaxed about this whole issue, but really he was more than a little wary of dealing with The Hatchet Mob. Having faced off against numerous rival gangs and drug dealers in Manchester and in Sydney before, however, he did believe he could handle this himself.

All he had to do was walk into Spice, make himself known to the waiting predators and put a hurting on them they would not forget. Then he just had to make sure he walked out alive.

Chapter Eight

Spice nightclub was already fairly busy, especially considering how early in the night it was. The early bird catches the worm though, or in this case, the early bird catches the hatchet.

As he made his way into the club, John had his head on a swivel. Not in an obvious way - one of the many advantages of all his training in boxing, Thai boxing and judo, was a very highly developed sense of peripheral vision.

Spice was a notorious drug den and had a history of violence. It wasn't what people in Belfast would have called 'a dive', however.

The club was decorated in a flashy and almost glamorous way and the clientele didn't look too shabby either - in terms of how they were dressed anyway.

There was no doubt they were using; it was obvious to anyone who understood drugs and the drug scene. Everyone was high and some people were very high. The very high ones would be the key to putting this whole thing together.

All John had to do was pick a good vantage point, select a few revellers who were higher than a giraffe on stilts and wait for them to want and seek more drugs.

Of course, the highest people in the club didn't necessarily need more drugs, but they would definitely want more drugs. The drugs already in their systems would tell them so.

This is why there is no such thing as a drug pusher; drugs push themselves.

John focussed in on a guy who was already causing a scene on the dance floor, dancing like a sweaty tribute act to Keith Flint from The Prodigy. He was wearing a garish shiny shirt - soaked in sweat - which was also drawing attention. And he was high, very high indeed.

His eyes were like black saucepans and his jaw was in a kind of chewing spasm. He looked as if he was about to consume his own head.

John knew that this guy wouldn't make it through much more of the night without seeking more drugs. As soon as he came down that one or two per cent from his euphoric state, it would be drugs o'clock and John would be ready.

He needed to spot these dealers and be sure. Not that he wouldn't be sure when the hatchets came out, but he wanted to control the situation as best he could. Knowledge is power.

He didn't have to wait long before the sweaty, shiny-shirted mess he had selected was off on the hunt for more chemical stimulation.

Even in his dazed and confused state, he still knew exactly where he was going. No doubt he was re-tracing his steps, going back along the yellow brick road to drugs.

He made his way up the steps at the side of the dance floor that led to a raised balcony type area.

There were loads of revellers up there, some leaning on the railing looking out at the dance floor, some engrossed in drug-fuelled conversation and some doing some more subtle dancing than those giving it their all on the dance floor below.

John just followed the guy's head and flashes of his shiny shirt, as he made his way through the crowd on the balcony area.

He walked right to the back and then disappeared, as his head ducked down from sight. He had obviously sat down - or at the very least leaned down - to do his latest little drug deal.

John kept watching and the head - attached to the sweat-drenched and garishly shirted man - re-emerged and came back into view, with an even bigger smile on its face. The guy had got sorted and John had found his dealers.

The members of The Hatchet Mob were at the back of the balcony area.

It was time for the next part of John's plan to kick into gear. He wasn't going to dwell on this all night. He needed to do what he was going to do and get an outcome, so that he could give Blair the go-ahead to send in his dealers. The Hatchet Mob had to go.

John made his way out across the dance floor, heading for the stairs up to the balcony. It was time to make a scene and get himself seen.

With the number of drug-happy punters at the top of the stairs, filling out the raised balcony type area, John was sure this part of the plan would be quick and easy. Certainly easier than the final phase.

Once up in the balcony area, it was time for him to get conspicuous - extremely conspicuous.

John made his way into the middle of the crowd and then started tapping party people on the shoulder and asking the big question.

"Pills or powder?"

"What?" would be the inevitable first response.

John would have to cup his hand around the person's ear and repeat his question at a higher volume.

By the second or third attempt, most people understood what he was asking and either waved him away - with a smile and a pat on the shoulder - or beckoned him in with a nod and a reach into their pockets for money.

In no time, John was knocking out pills and powder and raking in the Aussie dollars.

He was wearing his grey combat trousers and had a system worked out for ecstasy pills, cocaine, speed and money spread out among his many and large pockets. He had worn a smart looking short-sleeved shirt with his combats and some good looking trainers, so as not to fall short of the dress code and find himself turned away at the front door.

The combat trousers were ideal for drug dealing, especially in Australia, when he rarely wanted the extra layer of a jacket.

Of course, combat trousers were also ideal for combat. It was in the name. And combat was pending.

By the time he made it to the back of the balcony area, he had well and truly telegraphed his drug dealer status to everyone up there. The Hatchet Mob knew who he was, but now he wanted to know who they were.

Once he set eyes on them, there was no mistaking them. They were older than most of the rest of the crowd - thirties rather than twenties. And even though they had made something of an effort with their clothes, they still looked distinctly rough.

They had shaved heads, tattoos and well-developed muscles, shown off by their tight choice of t-shirts.

They certainly saw John coming and he made a point of offering drugs to a couple of people right in front of them. While on this occasion he didn't make any sales, they got the point. He had done enough to alert and anger The Hatchet Mob.

He could have moved on to the final phase of his plan right at this moment, but his inner cockiness got the better of him. John just couldn't resist rubbing their faces in it that little bit harder.

He walked directly towards them, making and fixing eye contact with the man he recognised from TV news and newspapers as Hatchet Willis, the leader of the gang. He went right up to him and sat down beside him.

As he sat down, Hatchet Willis quickly and instinctively put his hand over the trench coat sat directly beside him. The trench coat was right in between Hatchet Willis and the spot where John was seating himself. John immediately knew that he had found the location of at least one hatchet.

"You need any pills or powder mate?" he shouted at him, with a smile on his face.

Hatchet Willis just stared at him, seething with rage. This was not one of those occasions when the punter hadn't heard what he'd said at the first attempt.

John was tempted to shout it again, right into his ear, but at this point he had most definitely been made by The Hatchet Mob and made his point to them. He just continued smiling as his nemesis gave him a death stare, before winking at him and standing up.

As John turned to walk away, he knew The Hatchet Mob wouldn't be far behind him. Not that every member was there in Spice.

John had spotted what he believed to be two lieutenants there, along with Hatchet Willis himself.

They were there in person that night, most likely to make a violent point. Other members of the gang, further down the pecking order, were no doubt dealing in other nightclubs.

These other gang members and other nightclubs were not John's concern at this point though, as they were not encroaching on his territory. That was what mattered.

As John made his way back down the stairs and back across the dance floor, he could feel the eyes and bad intentions bearing down on him. The members of The Hatchet Mob were in his blind spot, but he could see them coming.

He made his way to the gents toilets, steeling himself for what was to come. Once he got inside, he would have a minute or maybe a little longer. Then the bathroom would become a blood bath.

NEIL WALKER

Chapter Nine

John made his way into the gents toilets and found them to be moderately busy. As ever in these situations, there were a lot of guys off their heads on stimulant drugs, hanging around talking like machine guns.

Especially in a hot nightclub like this, there was an extra buzz to be had from the cool air-conditioned breeze in the toilets; plus they got to hear the full, jabbering, drugged-up details of their friends and new friends upper-fuelled chatter.

All but one of the toilet cubicles were free and John quickly locked himself inside a vacant one. It wouldn't be long now before things kicked off.

As John leaned back against the door, preparing himself mentally for another war in the toilets of a nightclub, he was reminded of that night in The Doom Room in Manchester, in the summer of 2001. That was the night that changed his life in many ways; the night that set him on the path he was still following.

His first night dealing in The Doom Room seemed like a lifetime ago at this point, even though it had been less than a year and a half. All that had happened and all that had changed in him in that time made it feel like a massive era.

Unlike that fateful night in The Doom Room, John was waiting in the toilet cubicle ready for what was coming. There would be no surprise when he walked out to find himself under significant threat.

That night it had been an unwelcome surprise; tonight it was what he was here for, what he wanted.

These guys were a much more notorious and brutal gang than Ali and his guys had been in Manchester. John expected a tough test and would not be disappointed.

He opened up the popper button on his right rear combat trouser pocket and double-checked that the butterfly knife given to him by Peter was still there.

He confirmed that the butterfly knife was there and ready for use, just as the bang came to his cubicle door and the one beside.

"Get the fuck out ya cunt!" were the instructions from the other side of the cubicle doors.

John paused for a few extra seconds, to let the civilian in the cubicle beside him get out and clear.

When he emerged from the safety of his cubicle, he was greeted by a sight not too dissimilar to that which he faced in The Doom Room on that first night in Manchester. The toilets had been cleared and locked from the inside and he had three assailants waiting to do him harm.

Hatchet Willis stood in between his two lieutenants and slightly in front.

"Alright you cunt?" was his opening remark.

"Awesome thanks," John replied, smiling.

"You've got some bloody nerve."

"Sorry mate, have you decided you need some pills and powder after all?"

John was antagonising the situation even further, making a point of showing absolutely no fear and exuding confidence. While he was not completely fearless in this moment, he wasn't far from it. He knew he should be able to handle whatever they threw at him, although he might have to get hurt - maybe badly hurt.

Hatchet Willis had come into the toilets wearing the trench coat that had been sitting beside him when John approached him in the balcony area.

John had been convinced by the way Willis was guarding this trench coat, and the way it bulged as it rested on the seat beside him, that it contained the infamous hatchet and perhaps other weapons. The fact that he had come into the bathroom for this confrontation wearing it for effect, and perhaps practical use, just convinced John of this even more.

"You've gone wrong mate," barked Willis.

"Nah mate, you have," John retorted, unfazed.

"You've got balls like bloody beach balls, you little cunt."

"So I hear."

"Well me and my boys might have to cut them off for ya," Willis threatened, opening up his trench coat.

As he pulled it open, revealing the contents of both sides of the inner lining at once, John was stunned.

It wasn't just a hatchet, or a couple of hatchets. Each side of the coat had a number of sewn in loops of material to hold bladed weapons and it was evident that he had at least ten on him.

There was a small hatchet on each side, as well as two machetes and several assorted knives, that had up until now been concealed within the coat. They were concealed no longer.

"What do you think of my jewellery mate?" asked Willis rhetorically.

"Pretty," John responded.

He knew a response was not expected, and certainly not a casual, sarcastic response like this.

Hatchet Willis smiled, seemingly impressed by John's bravado. He then slowly removed his trench coat, walked over to the sinks at the side of the bathroom and draped it on one of them, with the weapons facing out.

He was taking his time, perhaps to intimidate John that extra bit, or maybe just to show that he had no concern about intervention or attention from the bouncers.

Willis then carefully selected one of the hatchets and removed it from its place in the trench coat lining.

"Choose your poison boys," he decreed to his two lieutenants.

They sauntered over to the trench coat - which remained draped over one of the sinks with the weapons facing out - while Hatchet Willis walked back to his original position in the middle of the gents toilets, facing off against John.

"Hurry it up lads, I've got drugs to sell," John taunted the three of them.

Again, Willis smiled at John's bravado and at his imminent intention to beat and cut it out of him.

"Won't be long now mate."

One of the lieutenants selected a machete, while the other picked out a hunting knife with one serrated edge and one smooth but razor sharp one.

The weapons gleamed in their hands under the bright strip lighting in the tiled gents toilets.

The two lieutenants made their way back across the toilets to their original positions at either side of Hatchet Willis, the only difference this time being that the lieutenant to Willis' left was level with him and the other lieutenant to his right was further back than before, in a more withdrawn role.

The lieutenant to the left was wielding the machete, while the one to his right had the hunting knife. John wasn't sure if their selection of weapons and the way they had lined themselves up across the room from him was something that they had planned, or if it had just happened organically.

Maybe the plan was that the lieutenant with the knife, in the more withdrawn role, was supposed to advance and stab the chunks of him that remained, after Hatchet Willis and his left-hand man had chopped him to pieces with the hatchet and machete combination, John thought to himself.

Whatever the plan in the minds of these Hatchet Mob members was, or if they even had a plan beyond attacking John with all the sharp stuff, the time was at hand for things to get very bloody.

Chapter Ten

"We're gonna carve you up," said the lieutenant at the rear, hunting knife ready for action.

John had the retort for this.

"You call that a knife?"

John pulled the butterfly knife out of his back pocket and skilfully spun it open, revealing the blade.

"This is a knife."

The Hatchet Mob all burst out laughing, both at the timing of the remark and in appreciation of the Crocodile Dundee reference, which they all of course got.

They were also amused by the idea that John thought his butterfly knife could rival their large bladed weapons.

John remained undaunted and was pleased that they were feeling overconfident. What they didn't know was that this was far from John's first time wielding a butterfly knife - very far from it.

John had owned a butterfly knife in Belfast for years and had taken the time to get well trained up in the use of it.

When he first got his butterfly knife, he had been unpleasantly surprised at how difficult it was to use. What had looked easy and cool in the movies actually required a great deal of practice, technique and skill.

After a lot of time, effort, cut fingers and rapped knuckles, he had in the end mastered the weapon. If John aimed to do something, he aimed to do it right.

Using a knife - and in particular a butterfly knife - was just another string to John's combat arts bow.

"You're a good laugh mate. What's your name?" asked Willis, as the laughter subsided.

"John."

"Well g'day Johnno! And where are you from mate? Bit of an accent there."

"Belfast."

"Belfast eh? Rough spot I hear."

"It can be."

"Yeah, well so can Sydney mate. And this is one of those times when it can be rough. And it's about to get very fuckin' rough."

John just smirked confidently in response, butterfly knife in hand and ready for the imminent violence.

"Well mate, we can't just stand here gabbin' all night. Me and the boys have got things to do. I have to say, I like your accent mate. Shame I'll have to cut your bloody tongue out."

The three members of The Hatchet Mob raised their weapons and looked ready to pounce. Just time for once last splash of fuel on the fire from John, before they would attack.

"So lads, all this talking. Is the idea to scare me or just fucking bore me to death?"

With that, the three muscular members of The Hatchet Mob came charging at John, fully enraged and thirsty for blood. Rather than tense up or panic, John just relaxed into it and let years of martial training take over.

Hatchet Willis and the lieutenant to his left would be the first to reach John, hatchet and machete raised to slice down on him.

John held his position until the last second as they ran at him, before swiftly dropping down on one knee in front of them, just as they got close enough.

With two unbelievably quick strikes, he thrust the blade of his butterfly knife first into the side of the lieutenant's right kneecap and then - having retracted the then bloodied blade with split second efficiency - into the side of Hatchet Willis' left kneecap.

The two of them fell to the ground screaming and bleeding through their trousers, their weapons crashing loudly on to the tiled floor of the gents toilets.

With hardly any time to spare, the other lieutenant arrived in front of John - who was still down on one knee - ready to thrust the blade of his hunting knife into John's neck.

In one swift and smooth motion, and again with perfect timing, John leapt to his feet, slashing the fingers around the lieutenant's knife and causing him to drop the weapon at his feet.

He then stumbled back screaming, with blood pouring on to the floor from his partially severed fingers.

In contrast to the shock, screaming, pain and confusion of his attackers, John was feeling relatively calm. He had a rush of adrenaline and was operating in a high gear, but he had known the outcome all along.

The confrontation seemed to be effectively over, although The Hatchet Mob may not have fully realised it yet.

John strolled over to the sinks, making a point of selecting the sink with Hatchet Willis' trench coat hanging from it, throwing it to the floor, before turning on one of the taps.

He began running his knife under the water from it and washing off the blood.

The two who had been stabbed in the kneecap were still writhing on the ground, moaning and screaming. The lieutenant with the injuries to his fingers was standing back, leaning against the far wall, and contemplating his next move.

"Liam Neeson says leave the blood on the knife. I like a clean blade though," explained John.

He continued to calmly run the knife under the tap water, rubbing the sides of the blade with his fingers to assist the cleaning.

John then turned off the tap, pulled out a paper towel and wiped it down. He spun it closed as skilfully as he'd opened it and turned to face the lieutenant who was still standing.

"What's it gonna be big lad? I've cleaned my knife and I'd rather not get it dirty again. Why don't you just unlock the door, fuck off out of these toilets and leave your girlfriends with me?"

He paused for a second, seeming to weigh up his options. Did he save himself from further injury and leave his fellow gang members behind, or stay and fight to ensure they didn't turn on him at a later date?

After all, Hatchet Willis was not known for his forgiving nature.

The lieutenant made his way forward, forcing himself through the pain barrier and somehow managing to grasp an empty glass beer bottle in his right hand - the same hand that John had already sliced. He had made his choice.

He cracked the glass bottle off the edge of the nearest sink, to create a savage glass cutting and stabbing weapon. He gripped this freshly made instrument of death as tightly as he could and set his mind to killing John.

John would have to fight for his life one more time, before he could attempt to leave the battlefield of these bloodied gents toilets.

NEIL WALKER

Chapter Eleven

The last member of The Hatchet Mob left standing, in the gents toilets of Spice nightclub, positioned himself opposite John, with only half of the deserted bathroom between them.

John did not re-open his butterfly knife, simply holding it in his right hand, closed and with the safety latch on. The safety latch end was pointing in at him and the rounded end, with the little bolts holding the blade in place, was facing out. The rounded end was the base of the blade and the little bolts were what enabled the butterfly mechanism to work.

Apparently, John did not feel the need to have the blade out and at the ready, as the last man on his feet came charging at him wielding a broken bottle.

Using broken bottles as weapons had been all the rage in Belfast, in the nineteen-nineties when John was a teenager. Some people would keep empty bottles under the table in bars, to avoid them being taken away by glass collectors.

Then, if there was a confrontation, they would pick up a bottle and smash the end off it against the edge of the table, ready to do some serious damage. Some guys would even decide which beer to drink based on the shape and size of the bottle, in case they needed to use it in a fight scenario.

The lieutenant raised up the jagged glass weapon, as he sped towards John with his right arm pulled back, as if he was about to bring it punching forward with the force and motion of a right cross, stabbing it into John's face. This was by no means the first time John had faced off against an opponent doing this.

As the broken bottle came flying towards his head, John parried the lieutenant's right arm away from him with his left hand and with a hugely powerful blow coming right up from his waist, smashed the rounded end of the butterfly knife - with it's jagged little bolts jutting out - into the side of his attacker's face with his right hand.

The rounded end of the folded knife impacted with such force on the lieutenant's cheek that it tore through the skin, smashing several teeth and catching him like a fishhook. His motion forward meant that the metal cut through part of his cheek, before snagging him in his tracks.

John swiftly pulled the folded knife out of his face, while slamming a short side kick into the back of his right knee, dropping him down on his knees.

He then brought the safety latch end of the butterfly knife crashing down on his nose. The nose shattered and exploded with blood, as the lieutenant let out a gargled shriek and fell sideways on to the tiled floor.

He was finished.

There was a lot of blood and a lot of screaming going on in that bathroom. John needed to get the job finished and get out.

He quickly ran his closed knife under the tap again and wiped it down with a paper towel, before sliding it back into his pocket. He then got down on his knees beside the closest lieutenant, still gargling blood and wailing, with blood pouring out of his head from both his nose and the hole in his face.

John quickly patted him down, taking all the drugs and money from his pockets. He then did the standard shoe check, pulling off his shoes and patting his socks. There he scored some extra drugs, putting everything into one of his combat trouser pockets.

He went through the same process with the other two, finding plenty more drugs and money.

Getting their drugs and money wasn't really about stealing it from them - although that was a bonus. The objective was more about taking these things from them so that they no longer had them, hurting their business and hurting their pride.

It was also an extra show of strength, to demonstrate how easily it could be done.

He searched Hatchet Willis himself last and even though he was injured and in huge pain, he still had plenty of fight left in him. All he could realistically do was talk at this point, however.

"You're fuckin' dead."

John laughed out loud and slapped him in the face, sitting down on top of him.

"I'll fuckin' kill ya," he continued, undeterred by the slapping, or indeed the stabbing.

"Are you seriously still trying to scare me? I would say you don't realise who you're dealing with, but you fuckin' do now."

"You're a dead cunt!"

John gave him one last chance to get the message and shut his mouth.

He pulled the butterfly knife back out of his pocket and held it over Hatchet Willis's face, still closed with the safety latch on.

He then began tapping Willis fairly hard on the forehead with the closed knife, speaking one word at a time, in between each tap.

"Don't…"

Tap.

"Come…"

Tap.

"Back."

Tap.

Not only did this not work, it seemed to further anger a now maniacal Hatchet Willis.

"You fuckin' cunt! I'll fuckin' kill ya! I'll cut your balls off and fry your fuckin' cock! I'll kill your whole family! I'll kill your fuckin' dog! You fuckin' little cuuuuunt!"

John could tell Mr. Willis needed an extra lesson and it had to be severe. It also had to be quick, as John really did need to hurry up and get out of there.

These toilets had been locked for far too long and John had no idea what arrangement The Hatchet Mob had with the bouncers, or who might be waiting for him on the other side of the locked door.

John made up his mind, flicked the safely latch of the butterfly knife open and spun out the blade.

"Wear this for a while."

He then held Willis' head down against the tile, with his left hand, and turned it sideways.

Into Willis' left cheek he pressed the point of the blade down hard and cut into it, from top to bottom. Hatchet Willis yelled as he was cut and he would be left with quite a facial scar.

John then spun the bloodied knife closed and with it still clenched in his fist, slammed a series of fast and hard punches into his face, knocking him unconscious.

John now jumped to his feet, rushed to the sink and rinsed his knife under the tap one last time. He wiped it down with a paper towel and put it back in his pocket once again. The vicious work was done.

All he had to do now was get out of the toilets and the club without drawing too much attention and without getting stopped, attacked or arrested.

Chapter Twelve

Getting out of Spice nightclub had been easier than he'd thought it would be. When he emerged from the locked gents toilets, all he encountered were eager, drugged-up revellers, itching to snort powder and urinate.

In seconds, he had made it out of the toilets and then out of the club through the fire exit.

He made a point of getting clear of the area in a hurry, before the full gory details of the violence that had taken place inside Spice were realised.

Once he felt suitably out of trouble, he text-messaged Blair giving him the signal to send his guys in to start dealing. He then made his way home on foot. His work was now over for the night.

The butterfly knife he had used had needed to be hidden in a stash box, for collection at a later time. John had done this, even though he felt like he'd made it safely away from Spice undetected.

John knew it was still too risky to walk around carrying a weapon he had just used in several instances of grievous bodily harm.

In an ideal world, he wouldn't have minded taking it home to clean it properly and then play with it for a while. It had been a long time since he'd used a butterfly knife before tonight and it had brought back some fond memories.

In Belfast he used to sit in his bedroom, spinning it open and closed again over and over, in much the same way that some people use Chinese stress balls.

Ditching it was for the best though and if Lisa had got up in the night to find him spinning a butterfly knife open and closed while staring into space, she may have found it more than a little unnerving.

As he wandered along the relatively deserted streets - under orange streetlights and the half-light of the moon - John was conflicted. Had he gone too far in dealing with The Hatchet Mob?

He had anticipated that they would live up to their name and turn up with the likes of hatchets and machetes to carve up their opposition; in this case - him. And there was no doubt that he'd brought Peter's butterfly knife with the intention of using it if necessary.

As the adrenaline slowly wore off and he reflected on the bloody scene on the floor of the bathroom as he'd left, however, he couldn't help but feel a little guilty.

In Manchester, the whole philosophy and power of The Brotherhood had come through the threat of and the use of extreme violence; controlling the fear.

John had been part of it too, until it went too far and his in-built sense of morality came into play. There was only so far John was prepared to go.

Those events in Manchester - which had come to a head at the start of this very same year - still haunted John to an extent.

And Doug's final words to him, 'You're just like me', echoed in his brain at times like this.

Doug had spoken these words like he really meant them, even though he was begging for his life at the time. John did believe that Doug had seen him as a kindred spirit and possibly even a young protégé.

Had Doug been right all along? Was he just as bad and just as capable of anything as Doug had been?

He had to rationalise though and keep his doubts and self-loathing at bay. On this occasion, he had brought a small knife to a hatchet fight.

He had inflicted bad injuries on the three members of The Hatchet Mob who had confronted him, but the injuries were by no means life threatening. If they had been allowed to have their way, he'd have been either killed or horrifically injured.

At the point where he had stabbed Hatchet Willis and one of his lieutenants in the kneecap, he had hoped he'd done enough.

The extra flurries of violence that came after that had left him feeling more like a cruel bastard than he would have liked. More like Doug, Sanjay and Simon than he would have wanted.

Although everyone in The Brotherhood had played a role in all sorts of horrendous acts, John believed that most of them had, in all likelihood, just been swept along and manipulated like he had been. On the other hand, he was sure that Doug, Sanjay and Simon had all had a sadistic streak running right through them.

He reasoned that he had probably only gone as far as necessary in Spice.

After all, he hadn't kidnapped anyone or beaten anyone to death. There had been no circular saw and bucket or harm done to anybody's loved ones.

Being the leader in his Australian gang did necessitate a lot more consideration of his perception than he had previously been used to. How people perceived him mattered greatly now, both inside and outside the gang.

Strength, confidence and invincibility had to exude from him at all times. Any vacuum in power could lead to injury, betrayal or death.

It was not that he didn't trust Peter and Blair; they had both proven themselves to be extremely reliable and trustworthy.

Without them, the gang would never have been the size it was or had the scope that it did. They were key to his whole operation and kept him insulated from a lot of the inevitable risk of the drug business.

He owed it to them to be strong; their fearless leader. And that night, he had been exactly that.

He knew that Peter, and Blair in particular, would be impressed with how he had handled The Hatchet Mob situation. He now hoped that would be the last they all heard of them.

This kind of scenario was something he hoped would be completely in his past soon enough.

In two more months he aimed to be home free, starting a new and amazing life with Lisa. The world would be their oyster.

John wasn't sure if Lisa would be asleep as he arrived at the front door of their apartment, so he made a point of being very quiet as he took the keys from his pocket and gently opened the door.

As he slowly pushed it open, he saw that the lights were out and imagined that Lisa had shut down for the night and turned everything off.

He pushed the door open further - his eyes adjusting to the darkness within - and he reached to his left to turn on the light. As he did so, he felt hands roughly grab him by the arm.

From behind the open door came a plastic bag that was quickly slipped over his head.

NEIL WALKER

Chapter Thirteen

John was trailed to ground by several sets of determined arms, not to mention the plastic bag that someone was holding tightly around his head. Then the blows began, as he felt himself being relentlessly battered with blunt objects.

He was trying to yell out, but he was being suffocated and could barely even breathe. The panic and pain quickly intensified.

The door had slammed shut behind them before the beating began and now that John had been thoroughly tenderised and was almost dead from suffocation, the lights came on.

Three bodies sat on top of him and the plastic bag was removed from his head.

He frantically gasped for breath, as he could finally get air. Breathing was still not easy, with the weight of three big guys bearing down on him.

As John turned his head to see who had switched on the lights, his heart sank. He saw a face from his past that he had hoped never to see again.

It was Simon, who had been perhaps the most cruel and sadistic member of The Brotherhood when he was in Manchester.

"Hey Johnny Boy, guess who's back?"

Simon then nodded to one of the other attackers who swiftly pulled a strip of elephant tape from a roll, while still sat on top of John. He wrapped it tightly around John's head, covering his mouth.

"I can't believe you left without saying goodbye," Simon joked, with a smile on his face.

He nodded again, this time to all three of the attackers who were sat on top of John. This signalled them to pick him up, like a horizontal piece of meat.

They carried him across to the sofa and roughly taped his wrists and ankles together with elephant tape.

He couldn't even strike out at them in the couple of seconds his limbs were free, his arms and legs having been too badly beaten with what John could now see were baseball bats.

They sat him upright on the sofa, with one of them sitting at either side of him and another standing behind the sofa, pressing his weight down on John's shoulders to keep him in place.

There was no escape for John now.

"So, Johnny, Johnny, Johnny. You've been a bad boy," said Simon.

He came forward so that he was only a couple of feet from John.

"You may remember myself and your other brothers from Manchester. It hasn't been that long has it John?" Simon asked him.

John could not have replied even if he wanted to, with his mouth held firmly closed with elephant tape. Of course, John did remember them all very well indeed.

He had thought he had seen the last of them, after murdering Doug and Sanjay. That was supposed to be the end of The Brotherhood.

Instead, he found himself facing Simon, with Ben and Andy holding him at either side and Dave leaning down on him from behind.

He and Ben had been quite close, during his time in The Brotherhood. He had been friendly with Dave as well, although everyone had been fairly friendly with Dave.

Dave was a likeable guy and a shameless self-promoter. Even though he had been one of the Brotherhood members who could be found in Nathan House the least, he had always made his presence felt when he was there.

He had labelled himself B.B.B.D. or Triple B: Big, Bad, Black Dave. Given that he was a big guy and the only black member of the gang, the name had stuck and afforded him a certain level of celebrity and notoriety within the group.

Andy had been one of the members John had spent the least amount of time with. He had been a very close friend of Simon - probably his closest friend in the gang.

The more John had realised how sick and sadistic Simon was, the less he had spent time around him and by association Andy.

"I must admit, I didn't see it coming; none of us did. You sneaky little cunt," Simon continued. "Doug and Sanjay, cut down in their prime. I'm sure you thought The Brotherhood was fucked after that - cutting the heads off the snake. What you didn't realise, my friend, is that The Brotherhood was a three-headed snake. And now the last snake head is going to fucking bite you."

Simon waved his finger at Andy, who immediately ripped the sleeve off John's short-sleeved shirt, on the arm he was holding, exposing his Brotherhood tattoo.

It was a thick black number one with the words 'all for' and 'for all' circling it.

"Well mate, I think we have to face the fact that you are no longer a member of The Brotherhood. And even when you were, I don't think you really took on board the meaning of that tattoo. So, as the only head left on the snake, I'm afraid I'm going to have to take it from you."

Simon then reached into his pocket, pulling from it his trusty Stanley knife. In Manchester, he had been infamous for its use in gang conflicts and territorial disputes.

John began trying to struggle as best he could and attempted to scream out through the tape. It was no good, however; Simon had him right where he wanted him.

Simon pushed the blade of the Stanley knife out almost as far as he could, giving him a good long blade to wield. He then walked right up to John, straddling himself across his lap, positioning himself to work, while further holding John in place.

He sliced the blade into John's arm, right above the tattoo and began to saw his way downward, sawing off multiple layers of skin, like he was carving a turkey.

Blood poured out of the quickly expanding wound and John writhed in agony, under the weight of his attackers.

Simon concentrated on what he was doing and carefully sliced across the bottom of the wound, removing the tattoo on one piece of skin.

As he held it up in the air for inspection, the slice of tattooed skin dripped blood on to John's head and shoulder. Simon climbed off him, proud of his work and admiring this freshly removed flesh trophy.

"There you go John, now isn't that better?"

Simon was smiling and in his element.

"Now that we've got that out of the way, I need a little information. Once you talk, we can be on our way back to Manchester and if you don't piss me off too much, we might even leave you alive."

Chapter Fourteen

"Now let me see," said Simon, looking through John's kitchen food cupboards and pondering.

"Yes, here we are!"

He pulled out a container of salt, followed by a small container of curry powder and another one of chilli powder. He then made his way back over to John and carefully placed them in a line on the coffee table in front of the sofa.

"So Johnny Boy, before things get really nasty, I just need to know where you keep your drugs and your money. Any answer other than a location will not be acceptable.

If you tell me you don't have any, you can't get to them, a dog ate them - any fucking lame ass excuse - I will just hurt you even more. If you want to talk, nod your head and one of the boys will take the tape off your mouth.

But if you try to be a clever cunt and shout out when they take it off, your mouth will be taped right back up and I'll be taking a couple of your fingers off with my Stanley knife as punishment. Do you understand me matey boy?"

John didn't make any sort of response, just staring at Simon with anguished contempt.

"Good," responded Simon, as if he'd had a positive answer.

"So, anything you want to say to me before we get under way? You could still make it easy on yourself."

John made no response and kept his head still, looking straight in front of him. Simon smiled and picked up the container of salt, making his way over to John.

He then slowly poured a large handful from the container into his right hand, just in front of John's face. John braced himself.

As Simon rubbed the salt into his big open wound, the pain was unbelievable. John had thought he was in a lot of pain after the slicing, but this was on another level.

The tape muffled what would have been bloodcurdling screams.

After Simon had finished with the salt, he made his way back to the coffee table and slowly went through the same routine with the curry powder, once again pouring out a large handful in front of John's face, before gleefully rubbing it into his wound. The curry powder was more painful still.

As Simon made his way back to the coffee table for the chilli powder, John was reminded of the guy in the Moss Side area of Manchester that he and Simon had helped Doug work on. They had held him down, while Doug slowly tortured him to death with a circular saw; Gordon was his name.

At the time, John couldn't believe that the guy wouldn't just talk and stop the agony. Now that he found himself in a similar position, however, John resolved that he wouldn't give Simon the satisfaction of telling him what he wanted to know and steeled himself for further pain.

He reasoned that if Simon was planning to kill him, he was going to do it whether he talked or not.

The pain from the chilli powder was almost unbearable. John wasn't sure if it was the cumulative effect of all of the previous painful traumas on the same area of flesh, or if Simon had saved the best for last.

As Simon stepped away from him again, John was agonised and exhausted. Unfortunately for him, worse was yet to come.

"You haven't let me down John. I knew you'd be a tough nut to crack. I'll bet you're sitting there right now, thinking something about how you won't talk, no matter what, and how you won't give me the satisfaction."

Simon was right, but John didn't react.

"Well, let's see if this changes your mind. Lads, turn him sideways and sit on the cunt."

The three gang members lay John down on his side on the sofa and all three of them sat their weight on top of him. They left his face exposed, so he could see but he couldn't move.

Simon made his way into the bedroom and John could hear some clinking, rustling and banging from within. Then after a few seconds, John's world collapsed.

Simon emerged from the bedroom with a choker type dog lead in his hands, dragging a stripped and bloodied Lisa along the ground on her hands and knees.

Her mouth was taped shut and a mix of blood and tears were streaming over the silver strip of elephant tape. Her body was covered in scuffs and cuts and there were noticeable trails of blood running down between her legs.

John was immediately overcome with guilt and by the horror of what he was witnessing. He was stunned, heartbroken and overwhelmed.

This was his fault. What had he done?

"We thought you were never coming home Johnny. Luckily, this little minx kept us all well entertained," Simon announced, grinning from ear to ear.

This brought some chuckles from the other three. John was completely sickened and furious.

"Let's see if this choker lead works okay."

Simon pushed his foot down on Lisa's upper back, pressing her flat to the ground and pulled upwards with the choke lead. Lisa's face immediately began turning red and it was clear she couldn't breathe.

After about fifteen seconds, Simon took his foot off her and released the pressure.

"Spoiler alert mate, this only gets worse. I can keep doing this for ages without killing her. Believe me, I had a good practice earlier on. And if you still won't talk…"

Simon reached into his pocket and pulled out the Sydney embossed Swiss Army knife he had purchased from Lisa that morning, folding out the corkscrew.

"Then I'll go to work with this. As it is, she is going to need a few stitches. If I really get going with this thing, she'll be left with a cunt like the Bride of fucking Frankenstein."

Simon had him. John was broken and couldn't let anything more happen to Lisa.

This wasn't about him anymore, or about his money, his pride or his rivalry with Simon. This was about Lisa, the love of his life.

He gave Simon the long awaited nod and Simon signalled to Andy to pull the tape off his mouth.

"Under the kitchen sink. False bottom."

Those simple instructions were enough and Simon was soon piling the fruits of John's illegal labours into a large rucksack. The other three Brotherhood members climbed off John and threw him to the floor beside Lisa.

Simon made his way over to John and knelt down in front of him, looking him right in the eye as he spoke.

"Live with this."

Simon then stood up and stamped down on John's head as hard as he could, turning everything to black.

Chapter Fifteen

The fold out bed was not the least comfortable bed he'd ever slept on, but it put him very low down to the ground. Anyone walking into his bedroom and seeing the bed made up for sleeping would have thought he was sleeping on a mattress on the floor; it was that type of fold out bed.

On the plus side, it did create extra space when he folded it up into a chair and the chair was comfortable enough.

The only problem with it was that it gave virtually no lumbar support at all, with the six inch foam back of the folded chair doubling as the fold out pillow area of the bed. It was really more in the realm of a bean bag than an actual chair.

Usually, John just left it in the folded out bed position and sat on it with his back against the wardrobe, for a little more back support.

The wardrobe, the cupboard, the wallpaper, the carpet, everything was the same as it had been whenever John had been living there growing up. The small bedroom looked like the late eighties or the early nineties had thrown up on it.

The only difference was the bed; his old bed had been thrown away when he had first moved out and replaced with the fold out chair bed, to create extra space. What exactly the space was for, John was unsure.

None of this mattered to John though. He would have hated the room and the bed if he'd had the will to care, but it just wasn't in him at this point.

The inadequate bed, the tiny room - which felt like it had shrunk since he'd last had to live in it - even dealing with his mother every day didn't matter.

She was still adapting to treating him as an adult living with her, rather than a child or teenager. He was numb to it all, however. Not comfortably numb, just numb.

The only thing he could feel, the only thing that got through, was guilt. Huge, grinding, never-ending, bottomless guilt.

Less than a year after he'd found himself lying on the grass in the grounds of Nathan House - trying to forget himself, overwhelmed by guilt - self-loathing was back on the agenda in a big way.

How could he ever get past it or forgive himself, after what had happened?

If anything, what had happened to Lisa in Sydney was worse than what had happened to Michael in Manchester and perhaps even worse than what had happened to Michael's mother.

Michael had been a fully fledged, sworn in, active and violent member of a drug gang. In fact, it was him who had got John involved with The Brotherhood in the first place. He knew what he was doing, what he was involved in and what the penalties could be.

Clearly, he couldn't have predicted or imagined that his mother would be dragged into it or the horror of what ended up happening to her, but he had involved her by association.

John had been out of The Brotherhood for some time, thinking he had taken them down as an active gang.

If he had still thought there was any chance that The Brotherhood could have remained a functioning gang or that they would have hunted him down in Sydney, he would never have allowed Lisa back into his life. She was too precious, too important to risk in any way.

That said, he couldn't allow himself to get off the hook. He was punishing himself, not forgiving himself or bargaining.

As far as he was concerned, he deserved it all: the pain, the guilt, the hopelessness and the suicidal thoughts - the full self-hatred package.

As he sat there that December afternoon, he stared out through the blinds at the low winter sun, partly hoping it would blind him.

In his right hand, he constantly spun his butterfly knife open and closed again, just as he used to when he was a teenager.

In his left hand, he pumped a forearm exerciser made of hard blue plastic over stainless steel. He had a softer one made with foam over the steel, but the hard plastic one hurt his hand; he wanted the pain.

His body was healed now. It had been a long process and he had come a long way physically in what was now almost two months. Mentally and emotionally he was still in intensive care.

The first priority for Lisa and him had been to get home to Belfast, as soon as they could appear fit enough to travel.

Obviously they needed a lot of medical attention and in Northern Ireland they could avail of it through the National Health Service. More than that though, Lisa had just needed to get home.

She had needed to spend more time in hospital than John, so he went to visit her every day. He wasn't sure if she was pleased to see him or not, but he had felt that he had to do it. And more than that, he had wanted to do it.

Everyone who visited her had noted that she wasn't herself. Even now, after all these weeks, she still wasn't herself.

John called over to her house to see her most days. It gave him a reason to get out of bed and get himself together - a reason to put on a front. He wanted to be strong for her, or at least to seem strong for her.

Although Lisa had not been very talkative and conversation between them hadn't exactly been flowing, as the weeks had gone by John had gradually explained everything to her. The Brotherhood, the drug gang in Sydney, what he'd done, why he'd done it, why he'd lied to her.

It probably didn't help. It certainly didn't help her forgive John or any of those gang members who had inflicted such terrible torment and injuries on her. But at least she understood now and could attempt to process the whole thing. That was something.

As soon as he was fit enough, John had hit the gym and started training again. Even before he knew what he was going to do, he instinctively knew training would help and would prove useful. It always had.

He was feeling lethal and even when he wasn't at the gym, he would sometimes fold up his meagre chair bed and in the small space of his bedroom he would shadowbox for hours. He would push himself, exhaust himself, and punch the anger out of himself, until he was a sweaty mess.

After all the healing, self-punishment, soul-searching and attempts to help Lisa in any way he could, now he had a purpose.

She had given him a purpose. And after that purpose came a reason. And after that reason came a plan.

The wheels were now very much in motion and the time was almost at hand. The thinking was done, the planning was done, the arrangements had been made and the airplane tickets and boat tickets had been booked.

It had all come from two words.

Lisa gave him two words that would define his immediate future; two words that had brought him back from the dead. Two words that had not stopped resonating through his head since they came out of her mouth.

'Get them'.

Chapter Sixteen

It was both Blair and Peter's first time in Belfast, not that they had seen much of it yet. They had gone straight from the airport to the gym for a workout.

Now they were back at John's mother's house and still running on the burst of alert energy that comes before the inevitable coma sleep of jet lag.

They had been fed on stew and protein shakes and were now reclined on John's folded out chair bed, with a box of beer in between them. John was on a wooden chair, which he had brought up from the kitchen.

"Your mum's stew was great mate," complimented Blair.

"I'll pass on the high praise mucker, although it's actually my granda who makes the stew from scratch. My mum just freezes it in tubs and then defrosts and reheats it for unexpected guests or if there's nothing in the cupboards."

"Still, she did a great job on the defrost," joked Blair.

"And that was one hell of a reheat," Peter joined in.

"Cheers lads," John smiled.

This was not the ideal setting for a Christmas Eve drink, or an optimal set up for three grown men to stay in for a few days. They would make it work though.

Blair and Peter were not the type of people who were prone to complaining and all three of them had done the backpacking thing in Australia and stayed in worse conditions than this.

"So, how's business?" enquired John.

"Drugs are our business and business is good," Blair answered jokingly, although it was a matter of fact.

Peter sensed it was his time to take over and give a more serious and detailed answer.

"We did like you said mate. We cut all the powder we had left down even more and spread the pills around. Supplies are low now, but our guys still have a little left to get them through Christmas. The thing they've got most of left is coke and Christmas and New Year is the best time to shift coke, so that'll probably work out well."

"Cool, so your guys should be able to hold their territory?"

"We should have no problems mate," reassured Peter.

"Happy days. Like I said to you both, I'm not going to be getting back in the game, but I don't want to put you guys out or fuck with your business."

"Oh, it's no worries," Blair said immediately.

"Course not mate," added Peter.

"I appreciate that lads. And as I've said before, I don't aim to send you home empty-handed."

"Thanks mate, but that's not why we're doing it," Peter said sincerely.

Blair nodded his agreement.

John smiled in appreciation.

As the mood had turned a little more serious and the subject had been broached, Peter thought it best to get the necessary discussion of the horrific events that had happened in Sydney out of the way.

"How is Lisa doing anyway?"

"Her body's healed up, but she's still not herself."

"It was terrible what happened mate. Just the worst. I'm sure it'll take her a long time to fully get over it," Peter sympathised.

"Yeah. I've tried to see her every day and there has been improvement, but I guess it's going to take a bit more time to get her all the way back on her feet."

"How about you mate, how are you holding up?" asked Blair.

"My body is back to full fitness; maybe even better than ever. My head probably still has a way to go."

"You looked good in the gym, but like you say, it can be harder to heal your head," said Peter.

John nodded.

Peter then moved on to say something about the perpetrators of the Sydney attack.

"I just wish we could have got them in Australia; made them pay, before they got out of the country."

"We'll get them," was John's concise and confident reply.

"We could have brought more of the guys mate. They all wanted to come and help you out," said Blair.

"It's awesome that they said that, but we'll be fine with what we'll have going into this."

Peter opened up a can of beer and took a big swig, before burping.

"What exactly are we going into? I take it we've got a plan?"

"Oh yes. I'll talk you through it all tonight and tomorrow, in between the Christmas celebrations."

"Can we have an overview?" followed up Peter.

He was eager to hear what the plan would be.

"An overview?"

"Yeah, an overview."

"We're going to go to Manchester, get our hands on The Brotherhood, paint the city red with their blood and take away everything they've got."

Chapter Seventeen

Kate had been Thai boxing since she was nine years old and by now was, in her own words, 'fucking amazing at it'. She never let herself get out of practice and always stayed sharp.

Now she had no shortage of sparring partners and was always keen and available to take on anyone willing.

She even gave pointers and lessons to those for whom Thai boxing wasn't their primary martial art. Stuart was one such gang member.

She never held back when sparring, favouring a 'go hard or go home' policy in the ring.

As Stuart tried hard to advance on her, control the ring and control fighting measure, she kept him at bay and under her control with a series of hard and low side kicks.

It was more important than ever, in her mind, to show no quarter in the ring, as she was now very much a woman in a man's world.

At first, some of the guys and been unwilling to spar with her. This was possibly due to an old fashioned idea about how a man should treat a woman or a woman's role. Maybe they had been afraid they would hurt her.

Then again, it could perhaps have been out of concern that they would be beaten by a woman and made to look foolish.

Over time though, Kate had well and truly established herself in the ring, in the gym, in the gang and in the drug world. Everyone in The Brotherhood had long since accepted her and learned the value of both her brains and her physical capabilities.

She was one of them now - an integral part of a powerful and dangerous drug gang.

The gym in Nathan House had really impressed Kate when she first saw it and she continued to appreciate the amazing facilities, particularly the full size boxing ring.

She had been a competitive Thai boxer in her late teens, but now, in her mid-twenties, was in the best shape of her life. This was largely thanks to the facilities at hand, right here in the place where she lived.

Every day she could train and spar as much as she wanted. Even though only eight of the gang members actually lived in Nathan House full-time at that point, the rest would come and train in the gym several times a week. This as well as the time they spent there before and after dealing at weekends and on particular club nights.

Stuart was primarily trained up in western boxing, but had been one of Kate's most enthusiastic students. He was still struggling to adapt and alternate between the two styles - to find a way for his body to accept and use both.

The issues he faced were the fundamental differences between the two martial arts, which were in a few key ways completely juxtaposed.

Western boxing revolves around the concept of presenting a narrow target in a side on stance, with the idea being never to be caught square. Thai boxing was the opposite, with a square on stance traditionally adopted by fighters.

Western boxing tended towards varying lines of attack going straight ahead, from either side or coming up from below. Thai boxing used high arms coming with a downwards motion to block, attack with elbows or fists, or grapple opponents in close or against the ropes, to go to work on them with savage knee strikes and kicks.

Stuart was still at the point where he was getting caught by conflicting neuromuscular training: he had trained his body in western boxing for so long that the techniques and style had become like additional reflexes. Now he was learning a new style that was altering that, but he was an eager and determined pupil.

He lunged forward with a front kick aimed towards Kate's abdomen. She jumped back far enough to make him just miss, before jumping forward with a right elbow that Stuart just managed to block.

They were wearing protective headgear, as well as boxing gloves, but the elbow would still have been a brutal blow to receive if it had connected.

Kate followed up with a series of sweeping kicks, driving Stuart into one of the corners. She was hoping to get him boxed in and then grapple at his neck and drive knees into his ribs.

He could see what was coming though and reverted to type just in time, switching to a western boxing stance before advancing with several jabs with his leading left hand, followed by a right cross that Kate just managed to slip, as she was backed up into the middle of the ring.

She smiled, very much aware of what Stuart had done and why. She then halted him in his tracks with front kick to the shin.

Having stopped the advance of her opponent, she moved forward again herself with a flurry of punches and elbows, with Stuart doing his best to block, slip and parry as many of them as he could. She caught him square in the face with an elbow, bloodying his nose and sending him crashing on to the canvas.

Stuart lay on the canvas for a while, a little disorientated and taking the time to compose himself.

Kate stood over him, sticking her gloves under her arms one at a time to pull them off. She then dropped them to the canvas, looking on to see if he was okay.

She removed her headgear with her cloth wrapped hands, dropping it down at her feet beside the gloves and spitting her gum shield out into her right hand.

"You okay mate?"

Stuart didn't reply for a second and then set about taking off his own gloves and headgear, while still lying on his back on the canvas.

He spat out his gum shield before replying.

"I think so."

He then dabbed his nose with his finger to check the extent of the bleeding and damage.

"It's hardly bleeding; I'll be fine."

"Good," replied Kate.

She followed up with some encouraging words for him, to lift his spirits.

"You know you're getting better all the time."

"Cheers."

Kate nodded in response.

"You really are good. Maybe we should think about a more gender-neutral name for this gang, like The Personhood," Stuart said, smiling broadly.

He sat up a little to talk to her.

Kate replied, "Maybe if I keep kicking your ass like this, you should think about changing your name to Bitch Boy."

She then threw her saliva drenched gum shield at Stuart, hitting him squarely in the forehead with it. This made him laugh out loud, as he collapsed back on the canvas.

Kate climbed out of the ring, saying goodbye to Stuart in her traditional way as she made her way out.

"See ya later, ball bag."

This was an unusual way to spend Christmas morning, but then Kate prided herself on being an unusual girl. She liked to live by her own rules.

As she made her way through the large gym to go and hit the showers, she paused to look at herself in one of the large mirrors that lined the wall on the far side of the gym. Her body was in perfect shape in her mind and it was largely exposed at this point, ideal for inspection.

She was only wearing Thai boxing shorts and a short vest top. She was athletic and a little muscular, but hadn't lost her feminine curves and look.

Her hair was tied back in a ponytail, as always for sparring and training. She was a sweaty mess, but long ago had learned to accept this as a sign of a good work out and she knew that getting a good sweat going was an integral part of avoiding injury, when training in martial arts.

Her eyes were drawn to her upper left arm, as she admired herself in the mirror. She'd had her tattoo for months now, but she still enjoyed the novelty of looking at it.

It was a thick black number one with the words 'all for' and 'for all' circling it.

Chapter Eighteen

Kate made her way carefully through the majestic hallway, walking slowly across the polished wooden floors. She was wearing heels and a tight dress and was mindful of slipping.

Kate was fairly confident walking in heels, even though she didn't wear them very often. On this occasion, she had made a big effort with her appearance.

She wanted to impress Simon and wow him when she walked into his office.

The floor of the main hallway in Nathan House was notoriously slippy, however, and she didn't want to begin the Christmas Night festivities by going on her ass, before Simon had even had a chance to see her.

Plus, the last time she had fallen in that hallway, she had ended up with a bruise on her hip that lasted for over a week.

The majesty of this grand hallway was still not lost on her, with the chandelier hanging from the extremely high ceiling and the antiques liberally scattered around the place.

She admired her surroundings as she proceeded with care up the carpeted staircase. Kate felt that she had a lot to be thankful for this Christmas.

As she reached the top of the staircase, she remained careful and very conscious of her footing. She slowly made her way along the lengthy hallway, stopping at the second door and banging three times in a particular rhythm that signalled to Simon it was her.

"Come in sexy lady," came the invitation from within.

She entered the office to see Simon sitting behind the large wooden desk, leaning back in his comfortable leather chair and smoking a cigar, with his feet up.

After taking a drag on his cigar, he blew the smoke into the air in front of him and smiled to greet Kate.

"Come on in baby. The world is ours," he said in his best Tony Montana voice.

He took pride in his Scarface impressions and even though Kate was always the first to put him in his place if he got too cocky, she had to admit it was pretty good.

"It's Christmaaaas!" she declared.

She was going for a Noddy Holder impersonation to announce her arrival and open the door to Christmas cheer.

Simon laughed, getting the reference and enjoying the attempted impression. In his mind though, he was also thinking that his Tony Montana impersonation was way better than her Noddy Holder one.

She quickly crossed the sparsely decorated room, which had a bookcase running along one side of it and a couple of paintings on the wall - an ideal setting and lay out for Simon's office and private room. He was the king and the general now and this was where he plotted his criminal conquests, with the help of his queen.

Kate sat down in the seat facing Simon, the wooden chair with the padded green leather back, on the opposite side of the desk.

Simon tapped the ash from his cigar into a crystal ashtray. He then rested it on the edge of the ashtray, leaving it lit, and sat up straight, taking his feet off the desk.

Smoking cigars was something he felt looked appropriate for the boss of a drug gang and he had been smoking them for a while now. At first, it was mostly for the cool and powerful look he believed it gave him, but he had now acquired a taste for them.

He poured her a Hennessy from the crystal decanter sat in the middle of the desk, into one of the brandy glasses beside it.

Simon had first started drinking Hennessy in his teenage years, as a tribute to his hip hop icons. By now he had really acquired a taste for it, with the Hennessy going hand in hand with the expensive cigars.

Kate had not traditionally been a Hennessy drinker, but she had taken to occasionally drinking it since she had been with Simon. She drew the line at smoking cigars, however.

As he poured another glass of Hennessy for himself and passed Kate's across to her, he quoted the famous rap lyric he often used in this situation. It was from the Xzibit track 'Get Your Walk On'.

"I can drink a whole Hennessy fifth. Some call it a problem, but I call it a gift."

Kate laughed, more than a little familiar with these words by now, and picked up the drink. She put it to her lips and savoured her first sip of the night.

Before Simon sipped his, he reached it out to Kate to clink glasses.

As she reciprocated and the glasses gently tapped off each other, Simon took another drag from his cigar, before resting it back on the edge of the ashtray. Then he took the opportunity to give a brief toast.

"Cheers baby. Happy Christmas. Here's to the best year of my life. I couldn't have done it without you and here's to many more great years."

She smiled - blushing a little - and took another sip of her cognac.

"Thanks babe, I appreciate you saying that. I do try to do my best for us."

"I know," he smiled back.

Simon was always appreciative of Kate and genuinely meant it when he said he couldn't have done it without her. Kate knew this and she valued him too.

Their relationship and the new life Simon had given her had been a revelation to her. She could not go back to her old life now.

"I hear you beat the fuck out of Stuart earlier," he joked. "Sounds like a real merry Christmas."

Kate laughed, retorting, "He does his best."

"You know, he used to be good mates with John Kennedy back in the day. The two of them were inseparable, when they were both living in this place."

Kate paused for a second to take this on board.

"Surprising. Stuart has never mentioned him, even when we got back from Australia."

"Yeah, I think he must have gone off him in a big way after the betrayal. I mean, I didn't particularly mind John myself, back in the day - apart from that accent of his. But once he killed Doug and Sanjay and tried to bring down this gang, he became number one on my shit list."

"Hey babe, maybe he did you a favour."

"How's that?"

"Well, you used to be number three in The Brotherhood. Now you're number one."

"Nah, you're number one Katie. I just try to keep up," Simon pointed out.

He was partly joking but partly stating fact.

If he was the king, she was the power behind the throne. He often told her that she was his Lady Macbeth, although he hoped not to end up the same way as the title character did in the Shakespeare play.

"No way Simon, you know I just love being at your side. Hopefully I'm a bit more helpful than Tony Montana's missus though."

"Fuck yes! She's a useless fucking nose hoover. You're the one who comes up with the plans, I just get this gang of fuckers to carry them out."

This was turning into a bit of a mutual appreciation society meeting, which Kate was very much enjoying.

While she tried to stay humble and give Simon his due credit - or even more than his due credit - she knew that she had been a major part of the rebuilding of The Brotherhood and that the gang would be nowhere without her.

Kate continued to praise Simon, to make him feel good and keep his confidence up. Plus, she was mindful of not creating any resentment between them, as even though she loved him, she knew the depths of his depravity and the terrible things he was capable of.

"You tracked John to Australia. Without that, we'd never have got things up and running like this again. It was small potatoes for a while, till we got our big start by hitting him for everything he had," Kate pointed out.

"True babe, fair play. But after that it was all you: the surveillance, the timing and the planning. It was even your idea to use the girl to break him.

Not to mention the fact that it was also your plan for exactly how to snatch her, and exactly how to break her. All I had to do was follow your nasty little instructions, you naughty girl."

Simon made his way round the desk with his glass of Hennessy in hand, kneeling down beside her and kissing her passionately on the lips.

"I still owe you a good spanking, mister," she flirted.

"Oh yeah, why's that?"

"I told you to kill that bastard."

Simon laughed, enjoying her fun way of phrasing things, as well as her ruthless intent.

"I know Katie, but if you'd been there you'd have done the same thing I did. It was just too perfect, looking at him and his bitch lying there on the floor, like two fucked up crash test dummies.

The look on his face was priceless. I knew I'd broken him to pieces and the worst thing I could do to him was to leave him alive."

Katie smiled, but gave her traditional final decree on this subject.

"If I'd have been there, I would have cut that fucker's head off and given it to his little bitch as a fucking paperweight."

NEIL WALKER

Chapter Nineteen

Boxing Night in central Belfast was traditionally busy with revellers. While not everywhere was usually open, the places that were open did very good trade.

Everybody wanted to go out, get drunk and take drugs, once the traditional festivities were over.

As John, Blair and Peter walked through Belfast city centre though, the streets were still pretty quiet. The night wouldn't really get going until later.

John knew this, but they had made their way into town early for business, not pleasure.

As a helicopter buzzed overhead, Blair and Peter both looked up at it, while John was practically immune to the sound, having grown up in Belfast.

Even though Belfast was now a lot less militarised than it had been in the seventies, eighties and nineties, there were still a good few military and police helicopters regularly circling in the skies.

"Don't worry lads, they're not looking for us," John joked, as they continued along the street.

As they approached Chang Village, they passed a newsagent that was just closing up. The young guy who worked there was wheeling in a cumbersome placard advertising one of the newspapers, with the massive headline, 'ECSTASY KILLS'. All three of them chuckled at this, as they walked by.

Blair had had enough of playing follow the leader and caught up with John.

"Where are we going mate?"

"To take care of some business."

"Oh yeah, what business is that?" Blair persisted.

"We need guns," was John's brief and to the point response.

"And will they be easy to get?"

"Blair, this whole country is nothing but green fields and guns. What's important is who you get the guns from."

"How's that?"

"Well, if you get them from a paramilitary group - even if you pay them for the guns - then you owe them a favour. That means in a month's time, they could be at your mum's door, wanting her to stash a pistol and some ammo under her mattress for as long as they choose. That is no good."

"So who are we going to get the guns off?"

"A guy who owes me a favour."

Just as the conversation reached it's natural conclusion, the three arrived at the impressive entrance of the Chang Village restaurant. To Blair and Peter it looked more like a nightclub, with it's giant blacked out windows and large funky sign.

It was closed, but John approached the blacked out glass door and knocked it several times - hard.

Eventually, a well built Chinese man in a black suit answered the door, opening it only a fraction and looking out at John without speaking.

"We're here to see Mr. Lee," John announced.

The well built man didn't flinch or register that John had spoken with his eyes or face; he simply shut the door on them.

After around a minute of the three of them standing there, staring at themselves in the reflective surface of the locked glass door, the door opened again - this time wider. A smaller Chinese guy wearing an expensive looking shirt and trousers appeared at the door.

"What's up motherfucker?" was the greeting from him to John.

"Alright mucker," John responded, as the two shook hands and hugged.

"These are my friends Blair and Peter."

"Friends of yours are friends of mine. Come on in guys."

This was Ken Lee, an old friend of John's.

Ken spoke perfect English with a strong Belfast accent, having been born in Belfast to parents from Hong Kong. He also spoke fluent Cantonese. As John could not speak Cantonese, he was never sure if Ken also spoke Cantonese with a strong Belfast accent.

John had been in Chang Village many times before, but as they walked through the restaurant, Blair and Peter were struck by the impressive décor. It kind of matched the outside, in the sense that with a few changes it could easily have been turned into a glamorous nightclub.

Most of the tables were set and ready for diners, in preparation for when the restaurant opened later that evening. A few tables, however, were cleared of cutlery and napkins and were surrounded by enthusiastic Chinese gamblers, playing Mahjong.

These gamblers were engrossed in their games and did not even look up to acknowledge the three white boys - or as they would refer to them, gwai lo - coming into the restaurant.

As the four of them sat down at a table near to some of the gamblers, Ken reassured John and his two friends that they could speak freely.

"Don't worry, they don't speak English."

John nodded at him in recognition of this as they were seated at a round table, which was just big enough for the four of them. There was already food in front of Ken, as well as what looked like neat whiskey in a glass.

"You guys want a drink?"

The three looked at each other and nodded.

"Whiskey okay? Black Bush."

"Sounds good," John enthused.

Black Bush was the good stuff, as far as he was concerned.

Ken barked instructions in Cantonese at the well built guy in the black suit, pointing at the glass of whiskey and holding up three fingers. They could all guess the meaning of this particular piece of Cantonese dialogue.

"You hungry?"

Again all three looked at each other, before John piped up, "I could eat."

"This look good to you?" Ken pointed at his plate. "Beef brisket with curry and some fried rice?"

They all nodded enthusiastically and Ken shouted something else in Cantonese at one of the guys playing Mahjong. The guy gave some half-hearted Cantonese protest in response, before disappearing into the kitchen.

John was glad to see his old friend and was enjoying the hospitality that Ken always showed him. He knew that very shortly he would have to reveal the reason he was really there and he was beginning to feel a little nervous about this.

Getting guns from Ken was a key part of John's plan to take down The Brotherhood and if Ken said no, he wasn't sure what he'd do.

They needed Ken to say yes, if the plan was going to work.

NEIL WALKER

Chapter Twenty

John knew he would have to time and phrase his request for guns perfectly and do his best to persuade his friend to help him out. He didn't want to have to use guilt, or tell Ken the full story of what had happened to Lisa and him.

He knew he would have to tell Alan the full horrific tale when they got to Manchester; there was no way round that. This already meant that more people would know about the horrors that had befallen Lisa than John would have ever really wanted.

John respected Lisa and he knew she would want as few people as possible finding out the details of the abuse she had suffered, at the hands of The Brotherhood in Sydney. John would try to ensure this as much as he could.

Fortunately, John had done a big favour for Ken a few years previously and he had never asked for anything in return. John was hoping that if good will and friendship weren't enough to secure the guns from his friend, then bringing up this favour and calling it in would get them the firearms they so desperately needed.

"The food shouldn't be long," Ken reassured them, before asking John, "So, how have you been?"

"Up and down mate. Got back from Australia a couple of months ago and had a few things to sort out. Now I've got some business in Manchester; we leave on the boat to Liverpool tomorrow morning."

Ken nodded, beginning to eat his food. After a couple of bites, he took a sip of whiskey before responding.

"You're lucky to catch me. I was in Honkers for a few weeks there and just got back."

Honkers was a nickname for Hong Kong used by people from there, with them referring to each other as Honkeys. Ken had made sure John was well versed in all this stuff over the years, so he knew John would understand what he was talking about.

"So, are you just here for a wee chat?" asked Ken, suspecting that he wasn't.

"Unfortunately not mate. I need a favour."

"A favour. What kind of favour?"

"Guns."

Ken paused, with a forkful of food half way to his mouth.

"Why do you think I could help you with that? I am a restaurant owner."

John sighed.

"Is this one of those times where we have to tiptoe around a conversation, trying not to use the word Triads?"

The guys playing Mahjong may not have been able to speak much English, but they certainly understood the word Triads. A few of them looked over at John as soon as he said it.

"No such thing," Ken responded.

He went back to eating his food.

"Okay. I still need the favour though."

"Ask someone else. What about that shit hole estate you're from? No offence. Couldn't one of the community representatives there hook you up?"

John laughed.

"Maybe, but I'm asking you. And last time I checked, I think you still owe me one."

Ken put down his fork, sat back in his chair and took a big swig of whiskey.

"That favour?"

"That favour."

"I wondered when you were going to cash in that chip. What do you need?"

"I need .45 automatics. I'd say six should do it."

"Let me guess, two each?" asked Ken, smiling knowingly.

John smiled back.

"You guessed it."

"Still trying to be The Killer, eh John?" Ken asked rhetorically.

At this point, the food and whiskey arrived.

"I'll need three bulletproof vests as well mate. The cool looking discreet ones, not those big bulky old green ones you used to always see the cops wearing here. I don't want any vintage RUC cast offs."

As the well built guy was setting down the drinks, Ken waved him over and whispered something into his ear. The guy nodded, with a serious look on his face, and left through the front door.

"Will be an hour or two," announced Ken. "Do you fancy a movie after we eat?"

"Depends on the movie," John replied.

Knowing Ken as well as he did, and being fully aware of his superlative taste in film, he was confident it would be something good.

"Well, I brought back the special edition DVD of Bullet in the Head from Honkers. How about we watch that in the upstairs lounge?"

"Sounds awesome," John declared, speaking for the group.

Bullet in the Head was a favourite of John's. He was an avid enthusiast of all John Woo's Hong Kong 'heroic bloodshed' movies, largely thanks to Ken having introduced him to them.

While Bullet in the Head was not his absolute favourite from this outstanding group of films, he still loved it and was keen for Blair and Peter to see it.

"So John, before we fill our stomachs, is there anything else you need to go with your .45s and bulletproof vests?" Ken asked.

He was keen to sum up and get back to his food before it got cold.

John's reply was simple.

"Just a shit-load of bullets."

NEIL WALKER

.

Chapter Twenty-One

Simon had taken a long walk by himself around the vast grounds of Nathan House, trying to clear his head. It had worked to an extent, with the bracing wind and very low temperature having served to freshen up his mind and body. Now he was ready for more cocaine.

The previous night in Nathan House had been one of extreme excess in terms of a variety of drugs, including alcohol. Most of the gang had either been there from early on Christmas afternoon, or arrived during the course of the evening, having got their family commitments out of the way earlier in the day.

The parties that The Brotherhood had in Nathan House had traditionally been legendary, going right back to the early days of when Doug was running things.

Simon had been determined to keep up or even raise the standard, since becoming gang leader. Many of the gang members had commented that the previous night had been the best Christmas party there ever, so he was pleased with his work.

To aid their recovery and get them psyched up for working in the nightclubs on Boxing Night, Simon had opened up the screening room for a movie double bill of New Jack City and Scarface.

The screening room was a small-scale cinema within Nathan House that Doug had installed. Of course, Simon had inherited the screening room along with the rest of Nathan House, but he was keen to make better and more frequent use of it than Doug had.

He knew that by the time his fellow gang members were watching Scarface, the cocaine and adrenaline would be well and truly flowing through the group. This in turn meant that by that night, they'd be fully charged up with drugs and enthusiasm, ready to do some serious drug dealing.

Boxing Night was a massive night for selling drugs, second only perhaps to New Year's Eve.

Simon calculated that they would be most of the way through New Jack City or possibly starting Scarface, as he made his was through the main hall. The main hall of Nathan House was a huge room with a wooden balcony running right round above it, matching the flooring and wood panelled walls.

It was every young man's dream, with a huge widescreen TV with a PlayStation 2 hooked up to it, as well as a DVD player and a VCR. There were black leather sofas in front of the TV, as well as other comfortable and expensive furniture scattered around the hall. There were even a couple of La-Z-Boy reclining chairs at the far end of the hall, by the stereo and pool tables.

The main hall was deserted at this time, which was highly unusual. Simon struggled to remember a time when he'd seen it completely empty, apart from when he was first putting the gang back together.

Enjoying the opportunity for solitude in the main hall was not his first concern at this time though. His top priority was to urgently get some cocaine up his nose.

He had held out for as long as he could while he was out in the cold, so that he could really enjoy and feel the benefit of his first line of coke when he got back inside; and his first line would be a big one.

There was no one there to see it, but he held his arms out at either side of him as he walked through the last part of the main hall, like a football player celebrating a goal. It was not lost on him that all this was now his and that he now both lived in and controlled an absolute gangsters' paradise.

As he arrived back in his office, Kate was sat at his desk cutting out lines of cocaine with a credit card on a big flat mirror.

"Make mine extra large babe," said Simon as he entered. "Super-size me."

"No problem sir," responded Kate, in a mock American customer service voice.

She then pushed two of the lines she'd been cutting out together with the credit card, evening them into one giant line. She placed the metal snorting device they shared at the far side of the mirror as he approached and sat down, inviting him to inhale it.

Simon obliged with gusto, snorting the whole massive line in one swift and practiced motion.

As he put down the snorting device and sat up straight, still sniffing, Kate picked it up and quickly snorted one of the normal sized lines.

"Oh yes," said Simon.

He was very much enjoying the instant relief and recovery of his cocaine high.

Kate smiled as she sat up, pushing in each nostril one at a time and sniffing, making sure she got it all well inhaled. She had the jittery, smiley enthusiasm of someone who had been taking cocaine for hours and had not stopped for any sort of break.

"When do you want to do the silver platter thing?" she asked.

"I still don't know about that."

"What? I thought we discussed this."

"Yeah, but all that coke. Do you know how much that costs?"

This was obviously a rhetorical question, but Kate chose to answer it anyway.

"Yes, I know exactly how much it costs. But more importantly, I know exactly how much it's worth. We are thinking big time baby.

What it buys you in terms of loyalty, good will and status far outweighs how much you could get by selling it - or more precisely, getting them to sell it."

Simon listened quietly, having heard these points before and at heart knowing they were right.

Something about the idea of giving away a huge amount of cocaine just didn't sit well with him, however. Maybe this was the closest thing he had to a moral code, he thought to himself.

Drugs are not meant to be given away; they are supposed to be bought, earned, or taken by force.

"To be the king and to be treated like the king, you need to act like the king. Be the king baby."

Simon smiled and nodded.

"Only if you'll be my queen."

Kate smiled back at him.

"Of course babe."

"Are we good to go?"

"Yes babe, while you were outside I was getting it all set up; it gave me something to do with all this restless energy," she joked.

"Cool. Maybe we should get it over with then, before I change my mind."

"Only if you're totally sure babe."

"Yes. You know I trust your planning baby."

"I'm telling you Simon, this will have them eating out of your hand. Then, with the money they'll make tonight, followed by everything we've got planned for New Year's, you'll be a fucking god."

This seemed to energise Simon, who leapt up out of his seat.

"Come on!" he shouted enthusiastically.

He then leaned over the desk and took another line of cocaine; a regular sized one this time. Lisa followed suit and made her way across the room.

She stopped at the antique breakfast trolley with a silver platter on top of it and lifted the lid.

"Ta-da!"

Simon was simultaneously impressed by how good it looked and hit by just how much cocaine he was about to give away. He knew they had to go immediately, before he changed his mind.

"Looks awesome Katie! Let's go give it to them."

It didn't take long for them to wheel the breakfast trolley to the screening room. Kate had put the lid back on the silver platter, to maximise the impact of the big reveal.

They walked in wheeling the trolley, just as the opening interrogation scene of Scarface was getting underway. Simon signalled Andy to stop the projector, so he could give his speech to the members of The Brotherhood.

The whole gang was there in that room; forty violent drug dealers, collectively high on cocaine and other drugs. As the movie stopped, there was a groan of dissatisfaction from the group.

One of them yelled out, "Come on man! This is Scarface!"

Simon had the response for this, as he took centre stage at the front of the screening room.

"Fuck Tony Montana, we kill kids!"

This brought about a number of laughs, followed by multiple laddish cheers from the crowd of gang members. Everyone in the room had seen Scarface a number of times and immediately understood the reference.

"Okay lads, joking aside, I know that it's sacrilege to interrupt the great Al Pacino when he's in Scarface mode. I only want to say a few quick words.

It's been an amazing end to this year and we have worked together to bring The Brotherhood back from the dead. I couldn't have done it without you and the sky's the limit from here on out!"

This prompted more cheering.

"And so, in the spirit of Christmas and to show just how much I appreciate everything you lot have done, I've got a little present for you all. If my beautiful assistant will help me…"

Simon gestured to Kate, who was standing over the breakfast trolley. She responded by removing the lid from the silver platter with a flourish.

"It's snowing boys!" Simon shouted.

He held up his arms and basked in the ovation that ensued. He then waited for the cheering and clapping to subside, before saying one last thing to the gang.

"Next year is going to be our year boys. We're going to own this fucking city!"

Chapter Twenty-Two

Having picked up their .45 automatic pistols, bulletproof vests and copious amounts of ammo, John, Blair and Peter had got them safely secured and hidden back at John's mother's house.

With that out of the way, they had now entered into the recreational part of their Boxing Night in Belfast. They would be leaving for Manchester the next day, but they were going to make the most of this final night.

Having had a couple of lively pints in The Jewel Bar, following the screening of Bullet in the Head in the upstairs lounge of Chang Village and the roundtrip to John's mother's house, they had made their way to Vincenzo's nightclub.

Vincenzo's was a place they would be able to get out of hand in. This meant out of hand in terms of drugs, drinking and general behaviour.

It was an infamous drug den, although it got a reasonably peaceful and hedonistic crowd. It attracted the kind of people who were more interested in being on the dance floor giving it their all when the lights came on in the early hours of the morning, than fighting with anyone or causing trouble.

This was fine with John and his two Aussie cohorts, as they would be getting into enough trouble when they got to Manchester to last them a lifetime.

John had always liked Vincenzo's; it was his kind of place. The relaxed attitude towards drugs and the law in general went hand in hand with his own.

The place didn't even have a bar or nightclub licence, despite having four floors of various types of music with dance floors and five actual bars.

They managed to get away with trading on a restaurant licence, by giving each person a free slice of pizza when they paid in at the front door. It was good pizza too, as Vincenzo's did actually double as a pizzeria on normal nights during the week.

At the weekend and on nights like Boxing Night though, it operated as a nightclub and was all about drug-fuelled mayhem.

The very top floor played hip hop and was generally filled with either stoners, semi-discreetly smoking cannabis, or ravers, chilling out between dance floor visits.

The next floor down was the techno floor - this was where most hardcore ecstasy enthusiasts would spend the majority of the night, dancing like maniacs in the smoky techno darkness.

The floor below that was a little brighter and played a mix of funky house, retro funk and dance music.

The ground floor was separated into two parts, an indie disco and a tabled chill out bar. The tabled chill out bar area was where people would sit to eat their pizza during the normality of weeknights.

On club nights this part was where people would sit to drink, talk and enjoy the effects of their drugs in a more serene environment than the various levels of chaos contained on the floors above.

John, Blair and Peter had got themselves a table in this part of the club and were sitting drinking bottled beer, waiting to come up on the ecstasy pills they had just taken.

This was ideal, as they could sit and relax, talk and be able to properly hear each other and gradually feel the effects of the ecstasy pills washing over them. Then - when they could sit still no longer and the ecstasy enthusiasm and energy was bursting out of them - they would charge upstairs to one of the floors above and join in the dance floor mayhem.

There were wine bottles with burning candles in them on the tables and a relaxed vibe of sociable chatter throughout the place.

At this point in the night, there was always a live band performing at the front of this part of Vincenzo's; on this occasion, it was a local band John recognised as being The Serranos.

They had been kind of a big deal in Belfast just before he first left for Australia, with their 'Comedown' EP getting a lot of radio airplay and providing the soundtrack to many real life Belfast comedowns. John even recognised a couple of their tunes to sing along to, as the three friends sat back, sipping their beers and enjoying the psychedelic funk rock of The Serranos live.

The three of them were drinking bottles of Rolling Rock beer, prompting a beer related question from Blair.

"How come you never drink Guinness mate? I thought all Irish people drank Guinness."

"Yeah, the idea that all Irish people drink Guinness is a bit like the myth that all Australian people drink Foster's."

This remark was an affront to both Peter and Blair.

"Mate, fucking no Australians drink fucking Foster's; that's why we export it to everyone else," Blair lectured.

"Yeah, that was one of the very first things I learned when I got to Australia the first time. But here it is advertised as the quintessential Aussie beer!"

Blair shook his head, although he knew John was right. He just found it hard to accept that the rest of the world thought the taste of Foster's beer was the taste of Australia.

"So you never drink Guinness?" chipped in Peter.

"Well, I wouldn't say never; maybe the odd time, if I'm down south."

Blair and Peter both chuckled.

"You see, we would never ever drink Foster's," Blair declared.

John smiled and nodded his head, accepting this meaningless defeat.

"I knew all Irish people drank Guinness," added Blair smugly.

After another ten or fifteen minutes, the conversation was flowing nicely, as the effects of the few beers continued to wash over the three of them and the early effects of the ecstasy were starting to kick in.

The conversation was getting a little bit more serious and sincere as well, as The Serranos live music continued to soundtrack this prelude to a come up. They had even started to get philosophical in their chat, as the three friends debated the topic of morality.

"Is it too simple to just say bad people do bad things and good people do good things?" asked Blair.

Blair was aware that he was the youngest of the three and that John and Peter were likely to have more finessed and elaborate thoughts and theories on morality.

"I suppose you could call that a simplification of conventional morality, religious morality or whatever. For me, it is nowhere near reality," John replied.

"Oh yeah, so what's reality?" asked Blair.

John simply retorted, "People do things."

It could have just been the ecstasy really beginning to come up on him, but in that moment it seemed to Blair that this had just blown his mind.

"How about this one: sometimes good people do bad things because of circumstances," Peter threw out there.

This also blew Blair's mind.

Again, it could have been Blair's lack of life experience and philosophical contemplation up to this point being met head on by words of extreme wisdom, or it could have just been the drugs.

"Life is painted in shades of grey," said John. "Black and white, good and evil, is just a way to simplify life and make it easier for people to deal with. People love it too; that's why so many people go to church on a Sunday."

"You'll never get to heaven with that attitude," Peter joked.

This prompted laughter from all three of them.

John then got serious again, before he continued.

"Really though lads, I am done with holding back."

"What do you mean?" queried Peter.

"I've been holding back for years. Mentally I've been holding back since university; holding back my brain, doing jobs that I am way too smart for. Masking my intelligence. Physically I feel like I've always been holding back as well. Holding back from hitting people who are testing me or deserve it, or holding back when I do hit someone, worried that I might kill them."

Both Blair and Peter seemed bewildered by this statement.

"Mate, we've been working with you in the underworld in Sydney for months, and I think I can speak for Blair as well when I say that we've never seen you holding back."

"Oh you have, you just haven't realised it."

"So the hatchet job you did on The Hatchet Mob, that was you holding back?" asked Blair, in disbelief.

"They're still alive aren't they," answered John, only half joking.

Blair and Peter laughed a little, although both of them realised there was some truth behind what he was saying.

"From this point on, no more holding back," John continued. "I'm going to use everything I've got against The Brotherhood; all of my intelligence and all of my physical capabilities. I'm going to hit them with everything I've got."

His two friends both knew he was deadly serious, despite the drugs and alcohol.

"I know what you mean mate," Peter joined in, agreeing. "Sometimes if you hold back on someone, they mistake your kindness for weakness. Sometimes you've got to go all out, to show people that you mean business."

"Exactly," John reciprocated, "and I do mean business. This time I am on a mission of no mercy."

"Well, we'll be right there with you mate," Blair reassured him.

"Yeah," Peter agreed.

"Don't think I don't appreciate that lads. It means a lot to be. And that's not just the ecstasy talking. Although it is a little bit the ecstasy talking."

The two smiled, knowing that he meant it, but also well aware that the ecstasy pills were coming up on them like an impending tidal wave.

"Right lads, a toast before we bounce upstairs."

John raised his beer bottle and the other two followed suit.

"Tonight we live life and party like it's 1999, even though that was a few years ago."

The other two laughed, while holding their bottles in position for the impending clink of glass.

"Then, when we get to Manchester, we fucking destroy this gang of cunts."

Chapter Twenty-Three

They arrived in Manchester late on December 27th, feeling like death warmed up. Partying in Belfast had gone on and on, with the three revellers getting fully caught up in the sentiment behind John's declaration of, 'Tonight we live life and party like it's 1999'.

They had stayed in Vincenzo's until it closed, at around three o'clock in the morning, and then moved on to Jessie's Piano Bar - an after hours nightclub that went on until seven in the morning.

After that, they had finished off the festivities with a confusing couple of hours at a ketamine after-party, which took place in the house of an old friend John had bumped into in Jessie's.

They went straight from the ketamine party to collect their bags of personal belongings, as well as the bags of battle supplies they would need. This of course included the guns, bullets and bulletproof vests they had secured the previous evening through John's friend Ken.

Once they had their personal effects and their weapons, they had gone straight to the port to get the ferry to Liverpool. There was no time to stop to change, shower or sleep.

The reason for them getting the boat to Liverpool and travelling by rail to Manchester, rather than just flying direct to Manchester from Belfast was to avoid airport security. The security measures in place for getting on and off the ferry were virtually non-existent, making it easy for them to travel with an arsenal of weaponry.

They had a cabin on the boat and had been able to get some sleep onboard, so they could theoretically have been feeling worse than they were when they got off the ferry. Although between the three of them, they couldn't work out how.

The journey from Liverpool to Manchester was mercifully quick and they were soon walking up the driveway of a slightly run-down looking terraced house. It was the house that John believed to be the home of his lifelong friend from Belfast, Alan.

He had failed to bring the note he'd had with the address written on it with him, so with a slightly muddled and muddied brain, there was an element of doubt. John knocked the door anyway and hoped for the best.

He felt a huge sense of relief when Alan's familiar face revealed itself as the door opened.

"Alright mate," Alan greeted, before the two old friends embraced.

John introduced his two cohorts, once the embrace was over.

"This is Peter and Blair."

"Great stuff, come on in the three of you."

It was a student type rental property, but Alan didn't share with anyone. This meant he had plenty of room, as well as the all-important aspect of privacy.

He was the same age as John, but was still living the student life, as he was on track to become a lawyer.

John had always felt that Alan used his intelligence wisely and productively, in a way that he never had.

"Dump your stuff in the hall and come through and sit down," said Alan, showing them through to the living room.

The three weary travellers followed him through, after dropping their bags in the hallway, and collapsed on to the three-seater sofa.

It was not a particularly nice or comfortable sofa, but it felt like bliss to them. During the final part of their journey and as they had walked up the driveway to Alan's house, they had been feeling like their legs were about to drop off.

Alan sat on the chair opposite them, before quickly realising that he should offer them a drink.

"Sorry lads, anyone want a drink?"

"Please mate, think we could all do with wetting our whistles," John replied on behalf of the group.

"Cool. Beer okay?"

"Oh yes," John answered enthusiastically, mirroring the happy nods of the other two.

Alan went into the kitchen and quickly re-emerged with four cans of Stella Artois, still in their connected plastic rings, holding them out above the three visitors so that they could pull themselves off a beer.

They all did so and he sat down with the remaining can, ready to catch up with his very good friend.

"So mate, it's been a while. What have you been up to?"

"Fucking hell mate, how long have you got?"

"All night," Alan replied smiling, although he could tell from looking at the three guys in front of him that they would be far from capable of sitting up chatting for anything close to that amount of time.

"Well, I think when last we caught up I was just about to go off travelling."

"That was it mate, your backpacking adventures around the world."

"Yeah, well that was amazing; I saw so much incredible stuff and I made a good friend on my travels. We stuck together for a lot of it. Then I went with him to Manchester, coz he said he could get me a job."

"Wait, you were in Manchester?"

"Aye."

"You should have given me a shout."

"Well, there's a reason why I didn't. It has to do with the job my mate got me."

"Okay. What was the job?"

"Drug dealer."

Alan burst out laughing, but his laughter subsided as he noticed that none of the other three were joining in.

"Drug dealer?"

"Drug dealer. Well, technically a member of an extremely well organised, violent drug gang."

"Right...and how was that?" asked Alan, playing down his disbelief.

"It was pretty fucking cool actually, till it all got out of hand. The money was amazing and they had this incredible mansion type pad where I was able to live for free. Plus, we had access to all the top quality drugs you could ever want."

"And then it all got out of hand?"

"Yeah; really out of hand. In fact, fuck it man, maybe it was out of hand from the start - the lines have been kind of blurry for me for a while."

"What happened?"

John took a deep breath before responding.

"Well, there were murders, disposing of bodies, chopping up bodies while they were still alive - "

"Jesus!" Alan interjected.

"Oh, I haven't even got to the really bad bit yet."

"Right," Alan said, bracing himself for something insane.

"So things were already pretty crazy, then Michael - who was the mate I met travelling - betrayed the gang. They tortured him, raped his mother, buried him alive and filmed the whole thing."

"Jesus!" Alan exclaimed again.

"Even that is not the worst part."

Alan just looked shocked and didn't say anything. Meanwhile, Blair and Peter seemed pretty relaxed as they listened, having heard this anguished saga more than once before.

"The worst part," John continued, "was that I helped. I helped the bastards do it."

"Jesus."

"I know."

"What happened then?"

"Then it did my head in; I couldn't live with it. The rest of them seemed fine with it all, which just made it worse. I picked my moment, when just the two leaders were in the big mansion house, and I killed the fuckers."

"Fucking hell!"

"I know. Then I took their money and their stash and set up shop in Australia with these two reprobates."

Blair and Peter waved their hands in unison at Alan, identifying themselves as the aforementioned reprobates.

"So, you started your own drug gang in Australia?"

"Yeah, I got set up there and everything was sweet. We had an amazing operation and lifestyle. You should have seen my apartment in Sydney. Lisa even came over and we were going out with each other again and living together."

"Belfast Lisa?"

"Exactly, Belfast Lisa. Everything was amazing and I was thinking I could get my money up, get out and start a new life with Lisa. A life without all the drugs and violence."

"And then?" Alan asked, once again bracing himself.

"Well, it seems I underestimated the members of The Brotherhood I left alive."

"The Brotherhood?"

"Oh yeah, that was the name of the drug gang in Manchester."

"I think I've actually heard of those cunts."

"I'm sure you have. In their own way they're famous, or should I say infamous. So yeah, I was one of those cunts."

"Fucking hell."

"I know. So they hunted me down in Sydney and got me and Lisa."

"Got?"

"Yeah, it was brutal. I got really badly fucked up and I don't even want to talk about what they did to Lisa."

"What, you mean like rape stuff?"

"Rape stuff makes it sound less unpleasant than it actually was. They need to invent some sort of new more extreme word or phrase for what was done to Lisa."

"Jesus Christ! How is she?"

"Still not herself. I mean she's fine physically, but her personality still hasn't fully come back."

"I'm sure. So I'm guessing you're here to get these fuckers?"

"You know it. I'm going to burn The Brotherhood to the fucking ground."

"Well you can count me in."

"No fucking way mate. You've done plenty just by letting us stay here. Plus, I was going to ask you if you could drive us around, seeing as you've got a car and you know the city."

"Of course I'll drive you around mate, but if you think I'm going to sit in the car like a cunt while you three jump out and kick ass, you can fuck off."

"Mate, you're on your way to being a lawyer. We're three fucking gangsters and The Brotherhood are the type of gang who would torture someone to death for showing their face in the wrong spot, let alone what we're going to do to them."

"You're right mate, I am on my way to being a lawyer - which means my life is on its way to being piss boring. This is my last chance for this kind of madness and you know I'm capable."

"Oh fucking right I know you're capable."

"So am I in? Or are you cunts bussing it round Manchester, waging your drug war?"

John paused and smiled, knowing that Alan had him.

"You're really sure you're up for this and everything that it's going to involve?"

"Yep. What exactly is it going to involve?"

"Blue fucking murder."

NEIL WALKER

Chapter Twenty-Four

John, Blair and Peter were all still a little fuzzy and fragile the next day, as they pulled up outside an average looking house in the Rusholme area of Manchester.

Rusholme was well known for it's large Asian community and a carload of twenty-something white boys driving slowly around, looking out the car windows at houses, had drawn more than a few stares.

It had taken them a bit of time and effort to find the address, but after a number of false dawns and a bit of confusion, they were finally in the right place.

Alan was driving and he wasn't feeling too bad from the night before. He'd had a slight hangover in the morning, after the four of them had sat up drinking for several hours, but the food they'd stopped for along The Curry Mile had sorted him out.

The curtains were closed in the living room of the house and as they looked out at it from inside the car, it seemed as if no one was home. John was virtually positive it had not been a wasted journey, however.

"He'll be in there," he announced confidently to the group, as he removed his seat belt and swivelled round in the car seat so he could see them all.

Blair and Peter were in the back seat, while John had claimed the passenger seat and the extra legroom beside his good friend Alan.

"How do you know?" queried Blair.

"I know. I can feel it in my water."

"What?" the still curious Blair continued.

"These are the kind of cunts who'll be in there doing some notorious gangster, drug dealer type shit behind closed curtains on a day like this. They're probably still on a buzz from last night, hiding from the daylight."

"You sure you don't want us to come with you?" asked a nervous Alan, keen to protect his friend.

"No mate, no matter what happens when the door opens, you guys hold fast. Even if he pulls out a fucking AK and puts it to my head, you guys be cool and stay in the car."

The three gestured with nods of resignation to indicate a grudging acceptance of what they were supposed to do.

"If I'm not out in fifteen minutes, get the guns out of the boot and kick the fucking door in."

This brought a more enthusiastic round of nods from his three friends.

They obviously found the idea of him going in alone and unarmed far too dangerous and reckless, but at least the thought that they were only fifteen minutes away from storming into the house - all guns blazing - brought them some comfort.

Alan checked his watch as John got out of the car, to ensure that the prescribed fifteen minutes would only be fifteen minutes and no longer.

The three looked on uncomfortably from the car as John made his way up the garden path to the house.

The house was nothing special and needed work. The door was a pretty standard varnished wooden door - which could have done with a new coat of varnish - with a black metal knocker on it.

There was no doorbell, so John knocked three times hard on the knocker and stepped back.

It didn't take long before several locks on the inside were being opened and the door inched ajar on the inner security chain, just enough so that the person opening it could get a good look at him.

"What the fuck do you want white boy?"

"Ali. I'm here to see Ali."

"You want to see Ali?" the door opener clarified, clearly thinking that this was an unusual and poorly judged request.

"Yep."

The door closed firmly in front of John. After about thirty seconds it inched ajar again, while another set of eyes checked him out.

This time there was no questioning or further delay; the door quickly closed again, the inner security chain was taken off and the door came flying open.

It was Ali, with a look of furious intent on his face.

"You've got a fuckin' nerve!" he shouted, as he charged through the doorway at John.

John took a few quick steps back before stopping.

Ali swung an angry punch at him, a sloppy and heavily telegraphed overhand right. John could have blocked, slipped or parried it three times over in the time it took to connect, but instead he just ducked down his head slightly to control where the punch landed.

Rather than impacting squarely on his nose - where it had been aimed for - the punch cracked hard off the top of his head, just above his forehead.

John was an expert at controlling where he took hits. It came from years of boxing training and also lots of experience of getting into fights and violent situations on the streets and in pubs and nightclubs against multiple opponents.

Sometimes, if there were too many opponents throwing punches at once from good positions, there was no way to avoid getting hit. The key in such situations was to control where they hit you and time your own strikes perfectly to take down your opponents.

On this occasion, there was only one opponent and one who John could have easily bested, but that was not the plan. The plan was to take the hits, but at the same time, he wasn't going to let Ali open his face up.

Ali drilled another flurry of sloppy but powerful punches into the top of John's head, as he covered up and presented Ali with a limited target.

He could feel and hear the punches cracking hard against his skull, but he knew they weren't doing any real damage.

Once the punches stopped and Ali stepped back, John brought his head up again to face him.

Ali was a well built Asian guy with a shaved head, in his mid to late twenties. In fact, he looked like he'd been working out a lot since John had last seen him, as he was considerably stockier than before and had more visible muscle mass.

He also now had a carefully styled, thin beard that he had obviously put time and effort into grooming. Appearances were clearly important to him.

"Remember me?" asked John, smiling at how unnecessary his question was at this point.

"Of course I do, you cunt. What the fuck do you want?"

"I want to talk."

"You want to talk with me?" Ali repeated back in confused disbelief.

"Yeah, can I come inside?"

Ali laughed.

"Oh, you can come inside. I can't guarantee you're going to make it out alive though."

"Okay, shall we go?"

Ali had to admire the balls on this guy, even though he remembered him as a violent enemy.

"Come on then Irish, let's go in."

As the two disappeared inside, Alan, Blair and Peter could only look on with growing concern and anxiety. They continued to watch the clock, knowing only too well that they may never see their friend alive again.

Chapter Twenty-Five

As the door to the living room opened, the smell of marijuana smoke hit John like a sledgehammer. Ali and his gang had obviously been smoking in there a lot for long time, creating a 'hotbox' effect on the room.

The room was full of hard-looking young Asian guys, sitting around on every seat as well as on the floor. They all looked to be in their late teens or very early twenties.

There were powdered drugs, guns and knives all over the coffee table in the centre of the room.

John's prediction that there would be some gangster, drug dealer type activity going on in this house had turned out to be very accurate. Guns, knives, drugs and a room full of thugs. This was the sight that greeted him.

None of the guys looked pleased to see John and all of them looked like they wanted to do something about it. They were ready, willing and able.

"What the fuck is he doing here?" one of them shouted out.

This guy had clearly recognised John from their previous encounter in The Doom Room.

He got up and crossed the room to square up to John as he entered, the door shutting behind him. Ali went right across the room and sat down on the unoccupied single chair that was obviously his seat, leaving John to be surrounded by this pack of hungry young wolves.

"Still think you're hard, you fucking cunt?" said the guy as he squared up to him, pressing his forehead right against John's.

The other guys formed a mob right behind and at either side of this guy, closing in on John and giving him nowhere to run.

John did not plan to run, however, and looked remarkably unperturbed by the precarious situation he found himself in.

"I've got a proposition for you Ali," he announced, talking right through the head of the guy who had his forehead pressed up against his.

This guy was Raheem, another member of Ali's gang who John had met before and violently assaulted in The Doom Room. He was perhaps even less pleased to see him than Ali was and the way John had just spoken loudly into his face, with his words directed at Ali - as if he wasn't even there - had only served to antagonise him even more.

"Who the fuck do you think you are?" Raheem angrily growled into his face.

"That's a great existential question mate. Maybe we can discuss it later, but first me and Ali need to talk business."

Raheem glared at him as if he wanted to kill him, which of course he did.

"Business?" Ali clarified.

"Yes, business. I have an amazing business opportunity to offer you."

"I never knew you cared," Ali joked.

He sat back comfortably in his chair, lighting up a large, cone shaped joint. Once it was lit, he inhaled, held the smoke in his lungs for a couple of seconds, exhaled and continued talking.

"I don't know Irish, I think I might just let these boys chop you up and put you in a nice white boy curry. What are those ones you lot like: a chicken tikka or maybe a beef vindaloo? But instead of chicken or beef, we'll just throw in some Irish white boy meat. Personally, I've got the munchies and I'm fucking starving."

This was all the encouragement the angry Asian mob needed, as they all grabbed and grappled with John, trailing him to the ground. They pinned him down, leaning their weight on him, as Raheem stood up and walked over to the coffee table.

"Hold out his arms," Raheem instructed.

He selected the biggest knife from those scattered on the table and picked it up.

The knife Raheem chose resembled something from a butcher shop and indeed it may well have been something from a butcher shop. If anything, it was somewhere between a large butcher knife and a meat cleaver.

He walked over to John and kneeled down in of front him to gleefully show him the blade.

Meanwhile, the rest of them had followed Raheem's instruction and clamped his arms in an outstretched position.

"You're good with your hands aren't you, you fucking Irish cunt? I think, for our own safety and peace of mind, we're going to have to take your hands away from you."

With this, he stayed on his knees and adjusted himself so that he was leaning directly over John wrists with the knife. He then pressed the razor sharp blade down on the top of John's right wrist, pressing it just hard enough into the flesh that it drew blood.

"I'm gonna take your wanking hand first mate, coz you're such a fucking wanker."

He raised the large knife up a few feet, carefully keeping the blade in line with the bleeding mark he had made on his right wrist. This was so that he could crash it down with power and precision, dramatically cleaving off John's right hand with one swift motion.

Chapter Twenty-Six

John had first encountered Ali and his gang in Manchester nightclub The Doom Room. It was at the time when he was first getting involved with The Brotherhood.

On that particular night, he had been sent in alone to deal with them, as a kind of test and initiation. It was a test that he had passed with flying colours and he had firmly dealt with Ali and the two members of his gang who were with him that night.

He had faced off against the three of them, taken a hammer from them and beaten all three of his attackers with it. The three had been left crushed, robbed and ashamed.

All three of them had been strongly affected by what had happened that night and their egos had been severely dented, none more so than Raheem.

He considered himself to be the mad dog of the group and found it hard to deal with being taken down so easily, especially with three of them having been beaten up by one guy. Now Raheem had his chance for revenge and he was enjoying it.

Raheem was practically licking his lips as he lined up the large, heavy, butcher style knife with the cut he had already made on John's right wrist. He was going to cut off the very hand that had humiliated him with that hammer in The Doom Room.

He wanted to take it off in one clean motion, like some kind of medieval executioner chopping off a head with an axe. He didn't want to wound his wrist; he wanted to maim him.

As he raised the knife up, he was completely concentrated on the task at hand - the task of removing John's hand - and was careful to keep the knife level with the line of dripping blood he had made on his wrist.

Once the knife was just above his head, he summoned all his strength to power it through flesh and bone.

"Wait," interjected Ali at the last second.

"What?" Raheem asked angrily.

He continued holding the knife in chopping position for another few seconds.

"Wait a minute."

This was not what Raheem wanted to hear, but he respected Ali and was not going to argue any further. He put the knife down and put his head right beside John's to speak to him before he stood up.

"Next time, white boy."

Raheem and the rest of the group all stood up, giving John the chance to do the same. He gladly took this opportunity and looked quite shaken as he got to his feet.

This was about as rattled as John ever looked in these types of situations.

"Irish, take a seat. The rest of you, go and chill in the kitchen for a bit," Ali decreed.

"You sure you don't want me to stay?" Raheem queried.

He was obviously extremely unhappy with the way things were going and at the idea of leaving Ali alone with this long lost enemy.

"It's okay Raheem. I'm just going to let the man propose a proposition. If I don't like what he has to say, then you can come back in and cut his fucking hands off."

This seemed to please and appease Raheem, who promptly nodded and followed the rest of the group out of the living room and into the kitchen, closing the door behind him.

John sat down on the sofa, facing Ali, and took a deep breath. Ali stood up to pass the joint he had been smoking across the coffee table to John, before sitting back down in his seat again.

John took a big drag of this strong skunk joint and exhaled, before beginning the conversation.

"So mate, it's been a while," was his jokey opening gambit, bringing a chuckle from Ali.

"Yeah, but I remember you well Irish. You made a big impression."

"I hear you were inside for a while."

"In and out mate. The cops fucked up my arrest, so I barely got a chance to unpack. A bit of remand and a lot of time in the prison gym."

"I can see you've been working out since I last saw you. Keep it up and you'll be as strong as me," John joked.

They both laughed and relaxed into the conversation a little.

"You've got balls like water melons mate. What the fuck do you want?" Ali enquired.

"I want to hand you the keys to the city."

"Oh yeah?"

"Yep. I hear my old buddies The Brotherhood are back in business."

"You hear right. How come you're not with them anymore?"

John thought it best to answer this question with a show and tell. He first took another big drag from Ali's joint, stood up and passed it back to him.

He then took off his jacket, before sitting back down and rolling up the sleeve of his t-shirt to fully reveal the fresh and brutal looking scar on his upper arm.

Ali winced as he looked at it, before taking a drag from his freshly returned joint.

"That's where my tattoo used to be," John explained.

Ali nodded, taking on board that John was no longer a member of the rival gang and that things had ended badly.

"So you're out. Well and truly out."

"Yeah, I'm out alright; and I'm here to take them down."

Ali laughed at John's bold declaration.

"Oh, you're gonna take them down? Fuck me, well bell me when you've finished mate. Good luck with that."

John was not laughing.

"Look, I've got guns, I've got people and I've got a plan. I know their operation inside out and I'm going to use everything I know against them. I can do this."

"And what do you want from me?"

"All I need from you is a list of all the nightclubs the gang currently hold. Then I need you to have your guys ready to move into the clubs, once I run the rats out. Do you have enough guys for that?"

"Does the pope shit in the woods?" Ali joked in response.

This was his way of indicating that yes of course it was well within his capabilities to put the appropriate number of guys on standby.

"And how quickly can you organise?"

"When is it going down?"

"The biggest night of the year; New Year's Eve."

Ali paused for a moment, to reflect on and fully take on board what John was proposing. He took another drag from his strong skunk joint, before passing it back across to John.

"I can do New Year's Eve. One thing I want to know though."

"What?"

"What's in it for you?"

"Revenge."

Ali sniggered, clearly feeling John had more to gain from this potentially fatal action than just revenge.

"And?"

"Okay, it's like this. We take them down and put a hurting on them that takes them out of the game. We claim whatever they are holding: drugs, money, and guns. You get the territory. Sound good?"

"Yes it does actually. How many guys have you got?"

"Four, including me."

Ali laughed out loud.

"Mate, there must be thirty or forty of these guys and they are fucking lethal. How the fuck are you going to take them all out with only three guys for back up?"

"Three words mate; speed and surprise. They won't see it coming, and we're going to hit them so fast and so hard and move between the clubs so quickly, that before they can organise to react, they'll be busted up and you'll be running their clubs."

"Fuck me mate! I knew you had big balls that time in The Doom Room, but those things are fucking huge. How do you even walk around with those things between your legs?"

They both laughed at this remark, Ali having taken to the plan and to John, despite their chequered history together.

"Pass me that pen and paper?"

Ali pointed at a small notepad and a pen, sitting beside each other, partially buried under the drugs and weapons on the coffee table. John dug them out and passed them over to him.

Ali started writing, continuing to talk as he did so. John listened, while smoking the remainder of Ali's joint.

"As far as I know, they're holding ten clubs at the moment. It's not quite as big an operation as it was back in your day, but they're expanding fast.

They'll have maybe three or four guys in each place, as they are still getting a firm grip on the territory. How quickly do you think you can clear ten clubs with that many guys?"

"I'm thinking in and out of each club in five minutes, ten tops. Then we race to the next club and do the same. I'll text you after we've hit each one and you can put your guys in place."

"Fucking hell. You really think you can do it that fast?"

"We have to. It's the only way it will work; blitzkrieg tactics."

"What tactics?" Ali queried, unfamiliar with the term.

"Blitzkrieg tactics. It's the name for the tactics that the Nazis used to use when they wanted to take territory quickly."

Ali chuckled.

"So now you're a fucking Nazi?"

John chortled in response.

"Fuck no! Blame my History A Level teacher mate. It is a good tactic though."

"It will be if it works."

Ali finished writing and handed the pad back across the table to John, having completed the list.

John extinguished the dying joint in the ashtray on the packed coffee table, before taking a moment to read the list. Once he'd finished reading, he nodded his approval.

"Okay."

"So not long to go till we do this thing?" Ali clarified.

"Nope, a few days and we're a go."

"What's your name anyway Irish?"

"John."

"And you really think you can pull this off John?"

"Put it this way, on New Year's Eve, we either take down The Brotherhood or die trying."

Chapter Twenty-Seven

They parked the car in an alleyway not far from The Doom Room and Alan turned off the engine. John had reckoned The Doom Room would be a good place to begin, given that it had been the nightclub where he had started his work for The Brotherhood and that it was always a busy and profitable club for drug dealing.

Also, it had amused him to tell Ali that they'd be starting there, given their shared history with The Doom Room.

The four of them all turned to face each other, as they remained sitting inside the car. It was time for a final strategy meeting, before they started the clock on this race against time style mission.

"Everybody ready?" John asked them.

He was keen to judge everyone's level of confidence and enthusiasm at this crucial juncture.

"Yeah," was the universal and eager response.

If any of them were nervous, they were doing a good job of hiding it.

John had a digital watch on and was setting it to count from all the zeros upwards as a stopwatch.

"Okay, so I'll start this at the front door of The Doom Room and we want to be out of there and back in the car in five minutes, ten at the absolute most. When we get in, I'll spot them and guide you towards them. Then I'll pick my target and strike.

When I hit, you hit - and hit hard. Fuck them up badly and quickly. Then take whatever they've got. Search them as fast as you can and don't forget their shoes. We want money, drugs and weapons.

Ideally, we want to hit them in the toilets, but if we have to we'll take them anywhere. Once I move, don't hesitate and don't go giving a fuck about who's looking. The key is to move fast, act fast and get out.

Any questions before we start?"

Alan raised a hand.

"Yes mate," John acknowledged the raised hand and pointed at him, inviting him to speak.

"Can I bring in the nunchucks?"

John laughed that this was Alan's primary concern.

In Belfast, the pair had been legendary with their nunchucks. Alan had acquired two sets of them, despite the fact that they had been illegal in Northern Ireland at the time. He had given one set to John and kept one set for himself.

Just like they had done with everything else involving combat and fitness training at that time, they had put a huge amount of time and effort into getting themselves thoroughly trained up with them.

Most people failed to do this when it came to nunchucks and would end up cracking themselves around the head if they ever tried to use them. They would often find themselves having their precious nunchucks taken away from them by their opponents.

However, Alan and John had found that once you got fully trained up with them and could control them and strike quickly and with accuracy, they were an incredible weapon and a great combat leveller.

They had taken on groups of five and six guys with them and left them all bloodied and on their backs.

Alan was obviously nostalgic for this time in his life and keen to once again get blood on his favourite weapon. John had no problem with this, as he knew Alan was very proficient with them.

Also, John was confident that on the way into The Doom Room, the four of them would not be searched and the nunchucks would not be discovered. The bouncers at The Doom Room never searched anyone for anything.

"Yes mate, just tuck them into your jeans and you'll be fine. Anyone else?"

They all shook their heads.

"Okay then, let's do this."

The four of them got out of the car, making their way round to the back of the vehicle and standing beside the boot. Alan opened it up to reveal three sports bags; two of them were large and one was very large.

He unzipped one of the two large sports bags. This was the bag containing weapons.

He then pulled out the nunchucks from within it.

"John?" Alan asked, checking if John wanted to join him in some nunchuckery.

"No mate, I want to get some blood on my hands; bust a few knuckles."

"Anyone?"

Blair stepped forward for a rummage in the weapons bag, eventually settling on a hammer, but at the last second throwing it back into the bag. He obviously had a quick change of heart and had decided to start off the night going bare-knuckle, like John.

Alan zipped up the large, weapons-filled sports bag and tidied it into the boot, before locking up the car.

It was time for the plan to begin. They made their way out of the alley where the car was parked and took the short walk to the nearby alley where The Doom Room was located.

The entrance of The Doom Room was around the side of a building, down a grotty looking alleyway. The supremely tacky red neon sign still had the faulty M that John remembered, thus welcoming them to 'THE DOO ROOM'.

John also recognised the bouncer. He still looked the same; shaved head, goatee beard, bomber jacket, a bit shorter than John, maybe five foot ten, but big with it.

As ever, he seemed like he'd need a jolt with a cattle prod to wake him into action, should any trouble start.

He was engrossed in his newspaper and waved the four of them to go through the door. He didn't search them or even look twice at them.

They walked down the steps of the entrance into a fairly dingy hallway, with a doorway straight ahead into the main club area. They could see that it was fairly busy and the atmosphere seemed relatively lively for so early in the night.

This was pretty standard for The Doom Room, which attracted a very enthusiastic and dedicated brand of drug-fuelled clubber.

The main dance floor area was very dark, as they entered the main part of the nightclub. John was eagle-eyed the whole time, wanting to be sure that he spotted the guys from The Brotherhood, before they spotted him.

Nightclubs in general tend to be dimly lit, but even for a nightclub this place was dark, ideal for the clientele who were there for the music and the drugs, plain and simple.

The four of them made their way through the place in a tight group, the other three following John closely, ready to move when he moved.

This club was hot, as usual, heated up by sweaty revellers. They were not planning to be there for long enough to get a full sweat going though.

In a dark corner of the room - away from the bar and the dance floor - John spotted four familiar faces. It was them and it was time to move and get into action.

Chapter Twenty-Eight

John marched towards the four members of The Brotherhood with purpose, keeping his head ducked down to avoid them seeing him coming. The other three followed quickly behind him, Alan reaching under his jacket at the back, taking hold of his nunchucks, ready to use them.

The four gang members didn't spot John as he approached them, with his back up team behind him. They were probably too busy keeping an eye out for business, John thought to himself.

Two of The Brotherhood members were seated at the table and the other two were standing up and at either the side of it. One of them was sitting on a stool at the table with his back to John as he approached, while the other one who was seated was facing John, but not looking at him.

The two gang members who were standing up were positioned at opposite sides of the table, so that the four of them were in a kind of huddle surrounding it. They were effectively fencing it off from anyone other than paying customers.

As John got close, he could see that they had drinks on the table. When he got behind the guy seated with his back to him, John grabbed him by the head, smashing his face through the half empty pint glass on the table in front of him.

There was an explosion of glass, blood and beer, although the noise and screams were masked by the extremely loud, banging techno music that shook the walls of this seedy club.

Usually, drum n' bass was the order of the day in The Doom Room, but they were clearly going for something a tiny bit more commercial, in terms of the music, for the larger New Year's Eve crowd.

This first crashing action by John sent his three-man back up team flying out of the traps.

Blair and Peter dashed around the table to grab the other gang member who was seated, before he could fully jump out of his seat and start throwing punches. They pushed him back on to his stool and then tipped him backwards on to the floor to violently deal with him.

Meanwhile, Alan had his trusty nunchucks pulled out and ready for combat use. He made his way quickly forward to tackle the guy who was standing at the side of the table closest to him as he approached.

The guy managed to catch him on the left side of his head with a right hook as he closed in on him. Alan had been too engrossed in unfurling his nunchucks to cover up in time.

The punch landed with a stinging thud on Alan's left ear, sending him stumbling sideways. He stayed on his feet though, and came flying back with a savage nunchuck blow, swinging them in sideways from his right side. It connected cleanly with the left side of his attacker's head.

As the guy stumbled backwards, Alan closed down the space, spinning his nunchucks round so that they were once again in an attack ready position, with one stick in his right hand and one tucked under his right arm, the rope pulled tightly between them.

At the same time, the other member of The Brotherhood, the one who had also been standing as they approached, was charging John. The injured one with the glass smashed into his face had already collapsed in a bloody mess at John's feet.

The gang member attacking John was part way through throwing what would have been a skilled right cross, when John swept both his legs at once using a savage low kick with his right leg. This sent him flying off his feet and crashed his head with full force downwards into the side of the table.

Blair and Peter were pounding punches into the face and upper body of their guy, who was on his back on the floor. Blair could feel ribs cracking, while Peter made pulp out of his face.

Alan had closed his guy right down, so that his back was against the wall. When Alan let fly once again with the nunchucks, he couldn't get his hands up quickly enough to block Alan's lightning fast nunchuck blow. It landed full force on the bridge of his nose, shattering it and bursting blood from it.

John stamped on the heads and upper bodies of his two beaten gang members, aiming to do as much damage as he could in just a few seconds. Both of them were completely unconscious in no time.

Blair and Peter were almost finished with their guy, as Alan tucked his nunchucks back into his jeans and rained a brutal flurry of punches into the head his opponent. His nose was now all but a memory and he was already sliding down the wall towards the floor. The punches finished him off.

Alan and Peter then began a swift search of their ruined opponents, as Blair leapt up and made his way round to search one of the guys John had dealt with, while John searched the other.

In no time, they had pulled all the money and drugs from their clothes and shoes. One of them had a flick knife, which Blair deemed to be not worth taking. There were no guns on any of The Brotherhood members this time.

Having pocketed everything they could, they made their back into the chaotic crowd, many of whom had now realised what was going on. They used the crowd as cover, pushing them out of the way as they moved through them towards the fire exit.

John aggressively pushed the fire exit door open and the four of them quickly made their way out through it, slamming it closed behind them. They emerged into an alleyway and took a second to get their bearings and work out which direction the car was in.

Once they knew which way they were going, they ran out of the alleyway they found themselves in and back towards the car.

One club down, nine to go.

NEIL WALKER

Chapter Twenty-Nine

John had a carefully constructed plan when he was in Australia and he had intended to stick to it; so much for best laid plans. A lot can happen in two months and it most definitely had.

Now he had a new plan and he could still be out of the drug world by the time this night was over. There was a hell of a lot to do before then though and he would have to get a hell of a lot more blood on his hands.

John was elated as they drove away from The Doom Room, as were the other three. Alan was even finding it hard to concentrate on his driving, such was the huge rush of adrenaline they were all experiencing.

He found a way to focus and drove carefully, however, as sloppy driving could get them pulled over by the police. Getting pulled over by law enforcement was unthinkable under these circumstances.

John took his mobile phone out of the glove compartment and got to work text-messaging Ali. It was just a brief message, telling him that The Doom Room was down and next up was going to be The Casa.

John finished the short text-message and put the mobile phone back in the glove compartment. Ali could now send his guys into The Doom Room straight away and have the next wave ready to set up in The Casa, once John and his three cohorts had finished their work there.

The Casa was a large nightclub that had been made out of a converted warehouse in the late eighties. There was a huge space and dance floor inside, which was ideal for the large-scale rave events it hosted. It was another notorious drug den and another prime target for John to strip from The Brotherhood's nightclub portfolio.

The Casa nightclub wasn't too far from The Doom Room, although once you got into the immediate vicinity of The Casa, there wasn't really anything else nearby.

This little area of the city was a bit of a post-industrial wasteland of abandoned factories and warehouses, apart from The Casa, which was a former warehouse that was not at all abandoned anymore. This particular nightclub was a bit of a clubbing Mecca in Manchester and people were happy to go a little bit out of their way to get there.

Alan parked the car beside a nearby warehouse and the four of them got out. Alan locked the doors and made his way round to the boot.

"No weapons this time mate," said John.

He knew Alan well and could tell that's what he was thinking.

"How come?"

"We might get searched here and it's not worth the hassle. Besides, I wouldn't be surprised if the bouncers here are part of the operation."

Alan nodded his agreement, not too bothered with this recent development.

"No probs mate, sure the four of us are lethal weapons anyway."

The four of them laughed, as they turned away from the car and made their way towards their next target. It was time to hit The Casa nightclub.

There was no queue outside the venue and the bouncer waved them in without problems. Alan could have smuggled in his nunchucks if he'd wanted to, but he had already got over the minor disappointment of doing without them. He had now set his mind to using only his fists on this occasion.

As they entered the vast main area of the club, John was struck by how few revellers were there. There were some people there and it would have been a decent crowd by the standards of most Manchester nightclubs, but not by the standards of The Casa.

John had expected to see the place a lot busier than this, particularly given that it was New Year's Eve - a massive club night. As he looked up and quickly scanned the balcony that surrounded the main part of the nightclub, he saw that it was virtually deserted and there was no one up there he recognised.

He felt exposed as he made his way through the club and concerned that The Brotherhood members who were there would see him before he saw them. The other three moved in a tight pack behind him, just as they had done in The Doom Room.

As they moved around the edges of this huge open space, looking out across the nightclub and scanning for members of The Brotherhood or drug dealing action, they couldn't see anything or anyone. Blair was directly behind John and he turned around to face him, pulling him close.

He spoke into Blair's ear through a cupped hand, to be heard over the hard house music that was blasting from the speakers.

"Let's try the bogs!"

Blair nodded his agreement and signalled to the two behind him, mouthing the word, 'bogs'. They got the idea and followed John as he made his way to the gents bathroom.

John braced himself as he approached the door into the gents toilets. He knew there was a strong possibility that as soon as they walked in, the bathroom could erupt into violence.

He didn't pause though, as he didn't want to show any fear or caution to the three following behind him. He wanted his fearless confidence to be their fearless confidence and he forcefully pushed the door open and walked quickly inside, followed by his three partners in crime.

The toilets were covered with sparkling white tile and were obviously kept clean and in good condition, unlike the toilets in some of the shabbier nightclubs like The Doom Room.

There were not many people in there, but John immediately spotted the ones he was looking for. Across on the other side of the gents toilets, against the far tiled wall, were four members of The Brotherhood.

He knew all of them, but one of them particularly caught his attention.

It was Ben.

Ben - who had been one of his closest friends when he had been in The Brotherhood.

Ben - who had been part of the small group that had travelled to Australia to take revenge on him.

Ben - who had played a part in viciously torturing him and brutally raping and defiling the love of his life.

Now was the time for John to take revenge on him.

NEIL WALKER

Chapter Thirty

Ben looked up to see John enter the gents toilets of The Casa, with Alan, Blair and Peter in tow. John obviously caught his eye straight away, but if he was shocked or afraid he didn't show it.

"Cunts, out!" Ben shouted.

This was his way of signalling that it was time for the few civilians who were in the toilets to leave in a hurry.

They scurried past John and his cohorts on their way out, as the four of them lined up across the far side of the gents toilets.

John and his three-man back up team were each choosing their opponent. John was in no doubt which opponent he was selecting and Ben was only too well aware of this.

As the door closed behind the last civilian leaving the gents toilets, Ben spoke up, as he and John eyed each other with venom across the room.

"So Johnny Boy, it's been a while. How's the missus?"

John was blazing with rage on the inside at this remark, but maintained a cool facade on the outside.

"She's a lot fucking better than you're gonna be in a minute, you fucking cunt."

Ben smiled and did a mock shiver.

"You always were a scary guy John. I'd say you're far too tough for the rest of us," Ben told him sarcastically, before adding, "You're a real hard man. It's just a shame that you're a fucking traitor piece of shit."

"You say I'm a traitor. I don't."

"Why, what do you call it, Mister University Genius? Do you think you're some kind of Che Guevara freedom fighter? Are you the fucking good guy?"

"Doug and Sanjay got what was coming to them. The Brotherhood is rotten to the core and if I'd thought the gang could survive without Doug and Sanjay, I'd have killed the fucking lot of you."

"You've got a nerve. Doug and Sanjay got what they deserved? I'll tell you who got what they deserved: you and your fucking whore bitch."

"You're a little scumbag, you fucking rapist piece of shit!"

"You say it was a rape. I say it was a struggle snuggle," Ben joked, prompting laughter from his side of the room.

The four at John's side of the room were certainly not laughing.

"Let me kill this low life cunt," piped up Alan, who couldn't bear listening to any more from Ben.

Alan had known Lisa well when he and John were younger, living in Belfast. What had happened to her had sickened and angered him beyond measure.

"This cunt is mine. You can have one of the other cowardly fucking rapists," replied John, staring right through Ben as he prepared to move on him.

Alan nodded his agreement, although the two were not looking at each other. While John was staring holes in Ben, Alan was eyeing his own imminent opponent, as were Blair and Peter.

"You're the coward mate. Killing the man who gave you an amazing life and running off around the world with our fucking money, aiming to leave us fucked. What were we supposed to do?"

"I tell you what you should have done."

"What?"

"Stayed the fuck out of my way!"

With this, John went charging across the room at Ben, who immediately followed suit, powering himself towards John. Alan, Blair and Peter also set off towards their selected opponents, who advanced towards them at speed.

John and Ben reached each other first, with Ben raising his hands, aiming to explode into a flurry of punches at John's head.

At the last second, John jumped up and to the left. He then threw his weight downwards and to the right through his right leg, which he aimed at the side of Ben's left kneecap.

He crashed down his full body weight on to the side of Ben's kneecap, powering all the force he could muster through the bottom of his right foot. John could feel the knee give way as his right foot smashed into it and a loud snapping sound could be heard echoing through the tiled bathroom, along with Ben's blood-curdling screams.

No one had time to properly look at this and take note, however, as each man was immediately locked in physical conflict with his selected opponent.

Alan went charging straight ahead at his guy, throwing a series of fast chain punches at his head, as if to try and go through him. The guy did his best to block and parry them, but some were connecting and he was getting backed up towards the wall behind him.

Blair and Peter both became instantly locked in relatively even bare-knuckle boxing matches with their opponents. But these were not careful and controlled boxing matches, where the aim is to hit and not be hit. These were both full pelt, toe to toe, power punching exchanges.

John slammed a powerful right hook into Ben's temple, with him being effectively powerless to defend himself after the pain and shock of what had just happened to his kneecap. Ben went stumbling to his right as John quickly pursued him.

Just as Ben was level with the area of the toilets where the row of sinks were - on his right-hand side - John grabbed him by the collar and the back of the head and slammed his head face first into the sink below him.

He could barely have done it with any more force and there was an eruption of blood as his face smashed against the clean white sink, instantly spray painting it red with fresh, warm blood.

Alan had taken a couple of punches, before knocking his opponent out cold. Blair looked to have got the better of his opponent as well, as he slammed a combination of quick punches from a multitude of angles into his head.

Peter was still locked in a fairly even battle though and seeing this, Alan moved swiftly to help him. With one skilfully swift technique, Alan trailed Peter's opponent to the ground from behind.

Alan and Peter then began punching and stomping on the guy. He was beaten.

John wasn't finished with Ben just yet and hauled him up from the ground by his underarms, before taking him once again by the collar and the back of his head.

For a second time, he slammed his face with maximum force into the sink. On this occasion, he managed to smash his head right through the porcelain in an explosion of blood and white sink pieces.

An almost unrecognisable Ben lay in a pool of blood and debris on the tiled floor. Alan's guy was out cold and Blair finished off his opponent with a right hook, knocking him out.

The guy that Peter and Alan were pounding on the ground was still conscious, screaming and trying in vain to protect himself from the barrage of blows that were raining down on him.

"That'll do," announced John.

He felt that they had done enough and that their time in The Casa was up.

"Let's search them and get the fuck out of here."

The three instantly obeyed and went to work searching through the pockets and shoes of their vanquished opponents.

They got a good haul of money and drugs, although not as much as they had managed to get in The Doom Room. None of these guys had been carrying weapons.

The four of them pocketed their cash and drug bounty and were ready to go.

"Right, let's make like a ball and bounce," John instructed.

They all moved towards the door of the gents toilets.

John tried to pull the door open, but couldn't. He then tried much harder, putting an extreme amount of force into his pull.

The door was locked. It had been locked from the outside.

"It's locked! Fuck!" he exclaimed.

A feeling of intense panic now ran through the group, who then began collectively trying to batter their way through the door. Their combined efforts failed to yield success, however.

"Fuck!" John shouted again, unsure of what was happening or how to proceed.

The mystery of what was going on wouldn't last much longer, as the music from the main nightclub area stopped playing.

"You're all fucked now!" declared the only Brotherhood member still conscious in the toilets.

"Shut up!" Alan shouted back, even though he sensed the guy was right.

The guy did shut up and he just lay there on the floor, smiling to himself.

The reason for his smile of contentment was soon clear, as screeching feedback from the nightclub speakers broke the silence.

It was a microphone being plugged into the PA system and switched on. A familiar voice then spoke into it, at a volume they could all hear.

"Hello Johnny Boy. So glad you could make it."

John knew the voice instantly. There was no mistaking it.

It was Simon.

Chapter Thirty-One

John turned from the inside of the bathroom door to face his three friends and explain the situation, which he instantly understood.

"They've got us lads."

"What do you mean?" queried Blair.

He got the obvious meaning but wanted to know the detail of exactly what was going on.

"That voice you heard is Simon, the leader of The Brotherhood. He is out there and no doubt so are the rest of them. It's a trap and we fell for it. They've got us hook, line and sinker, locked in these bogs."

"But how?" asked Alan.

"I don't know mate. There has been fuck all time since we hit The Doom Room, so they couldn't have put this together since then."

"They knew. They must have fucking known all along," deduced Alan.

Like the rest of them, Alan was sickened by these developments.

"How though?" queried Blair.

John racked his brains, trying to figure it out himself. Then he hit on a theory that seemed right.

"Ali; the cunt must have sold us out."

"Fuck! I knew it was a bad sign when he started punching the head off you," said Alan.

"The cunt has done us. Brace yourselves boys; things are about to get hectic," said a resigned John.

Simon's voice came loudly through the speakers again.

"Okay Johnny Boy, we've got more guns out here than the fucking Wild Bunch and they're all pointed at that the door of those bogs. At the risk of sounding like a cliché, come out with your hands up."

The four paused to look at each other, as they heard the sound of the door unlocking from the outside. It remained closed though; they would have to open it for themselves.

"I'm really sorry boys," said John to the group, sincerely apologising.

He felt extremely guilty about the situation he had put his friends in, as well as feeling incredibly worried about what they would now have to face.

They emerged to set eyes on a sea of guns being pointed at them by some very smug looking gang members. They were now clearly looking at every available member of The Brotherhood - guns in hands - with the exception of those gang members the four of them had already put out of commission.

John recognised almost all of the faces, as he made his way out of the gents toilets with his hands in the air. The others followed behind, also with their hands raised above their heads.

"Johnny Boy Kennedy, come on down!" Simon declared through the microphone, in the style of a nineteen-eighties game show host.

John looked up to see him in the raised DJ booth looking down on them, microphone in hand. Beside him was a girl he didn't recognise.

This girl was of course the power behind the throne of The Brotherhood, Kate.

Simon put down the microphone, causing a thud through the PA system, as it was still switched on. He then made his way down from the DJ booth along with Kate, who was walking at his side.

The gunmen lined John, Alan, Blair and Peter up against the wall of the main nightclub area. There was no one in there at this point, apart from the four of them and all of the gun-toting gang members.

Simon and Kate made their way across the dance floor to join the angry mob.

"Search them and take back what's ours," was Simon's first instruction to his troops.

Four of them tucked their guns into their trousers, advanced on the four prisoners lined up against the wall and did a thorough search. Simon and Kate stood there looking on, the king and queen of The Brotherhood.

The four gang members conducting the searches removed everything from their selected prisoners' pockets and stepped away, placing the money and drugs they found on a nearby table.

"Okay, you can put your hands down," Simon decreed.

The four did as instructed, still looking down the barrels of around thirty guns.

"Well clever clogs, have you figured it out yet? How did you end up in this mess? How did the great John Kennedy end up getting played by Simon Pollack and his old pals in The Brotherhood?"

John didn't answer. There was nothing he could say that would be of any benefit to him and his friends at this point.

Plus he wasn't entirely sure that he had fully figured it all out yet and didn't want to speak up with his theory and be wrong.

"Well, you'll notice that all The Casa party people have partied off. That's what you call friends of The Brotherhood mate. We had control of this whole place tonight and everyone you saw was here on our invite.

They've been sent off to enjoy the rest of their New Year's Eve elsewhere, with a gram of coke, a gram of speed and five sweet little ecstasy pills. This is one of the many benefits of moving into club ownership. I always did like The Casa."

Simon was smug and grinning as he spoke, clearly very pleased with himself.

"I knew about your master plan in every detail and I knew you'd come here earlier rather than later. I guessed you'd hit either this place or The Doom Room first and then I got a text to confirm it.

Are you curious about that mate? Have you figured that bit out? In this little 'who done it' can you tell me who done it?"

John was now virtually positive it was Ali, but again saw no benefit in announcing his theory.

"Could the one who done it, and the newest member of The Brotherhood, please step forward!"

John looked around the club, thinking that perhaps Ali was somewhere waiting in the wings and about to reveal himself. Instead, what happened was much worse.

John was hit with a soul-destroying realisation as the culprit stepped forward.

NEIL WALKER

Chapter Thirty-Two

Simon had John right where he wanted him and was milking the moment and the situation for all it was worth. The fact that he had got the better of John, both mentally and tactically, was his favourite aspect of this head-to-head victory.

This pleased him a great deal because John had always been renowned in The Brotherhood for his superior intellect and tactical nous.

Doug had been a huge admirer of John when he had been in charge of the gang, and at the time Simon had rather resented this. He had been in the gang for a long time and proven his capabilities and loyalty many times over, before John had appeared on the scene.

In the end, Doug appeared to have underestimated John and believed too strongly in his sense of loyalty. Between them, Simon and Kate had been determined not to make the same mistakes that Doug had.

They both knew John was a force to be reckoned with and had treated him as such, when putting together and executing their plans in his regard. They had now managed to get John exactly where they wanted him on two separate occasions, on two opposite sides of the globe.

In order to successfully achieve this, they had needed to be clever and cunning and also have a willing co-conspirator. This co-conspirator was just in the process of revealing himself to those he had betrayed.

John was completely convinced that it was Ali and had already berated himself in his own head for ever thinking he could trust his old enemy.

He had believed in the idea that 'the enemy of my enemy is my friend', but had come to regret it, when he had calculated that Ali had been the one who had conspired to set them up. However, he had calculated wrong.

As John scanned the club looking for Ali to make a surprise appearance, in his peripheral vision he caught a glimpse of one of those standing in line with him against the wall taking a couple of steps forward. It was his friend and trusted comrade Peter.

As John spun round with a look of shock and disbelief on his face, Simon was even more in his element. He mimed taking a picture with an imaginary camera.

"Click! That's a Kodak moment."

Peter turned to face John, a little bit ashamed, but at the same time somewhat pleased with himself. He too rated John's intelligence and capabilities very highly and was happy to have outsmarted him, even if he did have a slight feeling of guilt.

"You didn't see that one coming, did you Johnny Boy?" gloated Simon. "Tell him why Peter. I can tell he's just itching to know why."

"I was number two, but I wanted to be number one. It's that simple John," Peter succinctly explained.

"Are fucking kidding me Peter?" was John's angry response.

"You are a fucking fair dinkum disgrace mate!" added Blair.

"Fuck you Blair! And fuck you too John! I was dealing drugs and had my own crew long before you ever landed in Sydney. Then in no time John Kennedy is King bloody Ding-a-Ling and his old mate Pete is playing second fiddle.

And you're a fucking idiot Blair! If you spent a bit less time with your head stuck up John's arse, you'd see he's just using us and taking the fucking cream for himself!"

"Peter, you were like my fucking brother man," John responded.

"Nah mate, this lot with the guns are my fucking brothers! I'm bloody sworn in and all. Now I can't wait to get that fucking sweet tattoo."

John was confused and bemused. He couldn't believe or fully make sense of what was happening or how it had all come to pass.

"How the fuck did you end up in with these cunts? You've never even been to Manchester before."

"Careful mate, those are my brothers you're talking about," he joked.

He then continued the explanation of his treachery.

"You're right though, this is my first time in Manchester, although I'd say it probably won't be my last. You see, The Brotherhood is going global and you're looking at the new boss of the Sydney chapter. I'm number one now Johnny Boy."

"You cunt," was John's resigned response.

"That's it Johnny, feels good doesn't it mate; nice and warm and fuzzy, like a big hot cock up the arse," Simon said laughingly. "Tell him how we did it babe."

This was Simon's signal to Kate to take over the verbal torment.

"Hi John. I'm Kate; pleased to meet you. Simon has told me so much about you," she said, in a mockingly well-mannered way.

Kate then dispensed with the comedic mock manners and took up the mantle of explaining John's nightmare.

"And when I was in Australia, Peter told me so much about you as well. You should treat the people working with you a little better John.

This wonderful guy couldn't wait to fuck you over and we couldn't wait to tell him how. How do you think we knew where and when to snag Lisa and where and when to grab you?"

This was an even more sickening revelation for John.

"It was you that gave them Lisa?"

Peter had known Lisa well and socialised with her and John on multiple occasions. He showed no remorse though.

"I gave them everything they wanted mate and now I'm going to be king of Sydney; Sydney's number one. At first I couldn't believe they left you alive, but now I'm glad they did. This is so much better, watching you squirm," Peter replied.

"So, in case you haven't gathered yet, this is my girlfriend and one of the most valuable members of The Brotherhood, Kate. I just know you two are going to get along like a house on fire," said Simon.

"Fuck you."

"Peter was feeding us everything we wanted, every step of the way. He is going to help turn The Brotherhood into an international franchise, like fucking Coca-cola. And you Johnny Boy, you are fucked," Simon continued to gloat.

Simon walked slowly up to John, passing through all the gunmen still pointing their pistols at him. Once he got right in front of him, he took out his Stanley knife and gradually slid out the blade until it was fully extended.

He then leaned his head in close to John's, pushing the tip of the blade into his face, just below his left eye.

"Now you're mine mate; now I get to have my fun with you."

Chapter Thirty-Three

Simon stared into John's eyes for at least ten seconds as he pressed the blade of his Stanley knife into the skin just below his eyeball, almost drawing blood.

Whether he was looking for fear or some sort of collapse in John's outer confident strength, he didn't get it.

"I could cut you to pieces right here, right now. But fuck that! That's far too good for you. Far too quick. This is New Year's Eve and you lot are the fucking entertainment!" Simon proclaimed.

Simon was going to get maximum value out of this. He had been looking forward to it for a while now and would enjoy it on a personal level.

He was also aware of the significance that killing John Kennedy and his friends would have for The Brotherhood as a gang.

Simon took his knife away from John's face and turned to face the enthusiastic crowd of Brotherhood members.

He then pointed with the blade at a few members and gave out instructions.

"Tape up John and the other Irish one. Leave the young one off Home and Away with his hands free. He's up first."

Up first; up first for what? John wasn't sure, but he knew it wouldn't be good.

"Strip them to the waist first," added Kate, "all three of them."

Simon turned to her and smiled.

"You dirty bitch," he joked.

"A girl's got to have her fun," she joked back. "Besides, it will give them less protection. I want to see them bleed."

"That's my girl."

Three gang members tucked their guns into their trousers and did as Simon and Kate had instructed, stripping all three of the prisoners to the waist and taping up John and Alan. Blair was left standing there topless, as the three gang members walked away.

Simon and Kate made their way back up to the raised DJ booth, obviously wanting to have a bird's eye view of whatever was going to come next.

Once back in the DJ booth, Simon picked up the microphone again and addressed the three prisoners, as well as the crowd of Brotherhood members.

"Okay boys, I think we can put the guns away now. Keep them handy though. If any one of these cunts tries anything or misbehaves, tickle their fucking kneecap with a bullet. As for you three fuckers, welcome to The Brotherhood's New Year's Eve party."

All of the gang members cheered, as they collectively put their guns away.

"Johnny Boy, as you and the rest of the brothers here know, we usually have the New Year's Eve party back in Nathan House. But this year, given that I've acquired this lovely piece of real estate and that you three muggy cunts have seen fit to drop in on us, we've got a very special party planned and you three enemies of The Brotherhood are going to be the stars of the fucking show."

This prompted another big cheer from The Brotherhood en masse.

"Does everyone here know what being lined up is?"

Simon paused to allow time for a response, but none was forthcoming.

"Well, just in case any of you don't, it's a well-named phenomenon that originated in American prisons. When they have a large number of prisoners sharing a big cell and a new inmate arrives, they line him up. That means that they get in a line in front of him and fight him one after another, until he is completely fucked up.

Now we get to have a New Year's Eve line up to welcome you three visitors to our new place, and your fucking death row prison cell. And we've got a lot of fucking inmates in line for you!"

The crowd went crazy for this bit, giving Simon a big ovation. They were clearly keen and eager to be involved in this particular party game.

The fact that they were all sworn in members of The Brotherhood and John was despised among them for his actions as 'the traitor' made it all the sweeter for them.

"So, you three bitches, fucking brace yourselves. We've got a lot of brothers here to take their turn and play their part in beating you to death. We've got all sorts of weapons and nasty surprises to keep it interesting, and a fuck load of drugs to keep us buzzing and up for it. And most importantly, we've got all fucking night!"

The crowd found an even higher level yet of noisy excitement to greet this announcement. Simon was giving them exactly what they all wanted. This was much more than they could have ever hoped for.

Not only was Simon raising their morale and giving them a legendary experience in The Brotherhood world, he was also cementing his place as the new king of the gang.

Chapter Thirty-Four

Simon's big plan for New Year's Eve was coming to fruition perfectly.

John had played right into his hands and taken his lifelong friend Alan and his friend and lieutenant Blair with him. It seemed like none of the three of them would live to see the sun rise on the first day of 2003.

It was time for Simon to address the crowd again, to give out instructions and get the violent proceedings under way.

"Right then, let's make a ring and put these cunts in it! I want to see gambling, drug-taking, drinking and a whole lot of blood!"

These words from their gang leader brought a final cheer from the crowd, as he finished speaking for now and they followed his instructions.

John and Alan were carried to a spot at the back of the dance floor and forced down on their knees. They had their wrists and ankles bound with elephant tape and were positioned facing the DJ booth, where Simon and Kate were still standing looking down on them.

The crowd then formed a sort of circle around the dance floor, which was clearly about to become the improvised boxing ring.

A few of them went to the bar and were bringing back bottles of whiskey, vodka and champagne. Others were cutting out a sea of parallel lines of powdered drugs on the tables around the fight circle.

Blair was already in the ring area, with two Brotherhood members holding him and a third with a gun in his back. He would be the first to be 'lined up'.

A couple of them carried in a large plastic container and put it in the corner beside the raised DJ booth where Simon and Kate were. This was clearly to be the 'home' corner of this improvised boxing ring.

The plastic container was filled with a variety of nasty looking weapons. John, Alan and Blair could all see this, as some of the weapons were sticking out at the top.

This was going to be carnage.

John imagined he would not be up until after his two friends had been put through their ordeals in the ring. He believed they would save the best for last.

At this point, John was far more concerned about his friends than he was about himself.

Blair had been trained up to a good standard in boxing and combat when John had met him. John had then trained him up to an even higher level, but this was going to be a ridiculously stern test.

Alan was one of the toughest guys he'd ever known and had a similar martial training background to John. While he had been out of the game for a while, John had higher hopes for him than he did for Blair.

As for himself, in a way he was looking forward to it. He'd been wanting to get his hands on these guys for months and now they were going to present themselves to him.

Granted, he was unlikely to be given an even chance, or what people in Belfast would have referred to as a 'fair dig'.

The members of The Brotherhood would come at him in pairs, in groups, with weapons. He would be blasted with everything they had.

John still relished the prospect of hurting them - of getting more of their blood on his hands. The only one he wasn't particularly eager to tear limb from limb was Stuart, who he had noticed in the crowd.

They had been like best friends when he was in The Brotherhood and Stuart had never really wronged him directly.

In fact, John believed that Stuart had been swept along by the gang in much the same way as he had been. Indeed, he had actually been the one to warn John about Simon and his sadism, when John had first joined The Brotherhood.

John was sure that Stuart would not have approved of or enjoyed the thought of what had happened to Lisa and him.

If it came to it though, John would hurt him just as he would any of the rest of them. If Stuart was in his way, he would have to get out of his way.

As John sat there on his knees, watching this macabre spectacle about to unfold, his thoughts turned briefly to the four members of The Brotherhood lying bleeding on the floor of the gents toilets. John may have missed it, but as far as he was aware no one had even mentioned them or gone in to check on them.

They appeared to have just been left there; left to bleed and possibly even die. Ben could well have been dead already.

The Brotherhood was still the same group of selfish cunts claiming to be brothers, thought John.

He supposed that if they did die, the gang members' bodies would be part of the very same clean up operation as the bodies of himself and his two friends. He knew how these things worked; he had done his fair share of 'cleaning up' when he was in The Brotherhood.

No trace would be left of the violence that had occurred in this place. No bodies would ever be found. They would all be discretely buried and forgotten about.

The only mercy for them now would be the sweet release of death.

Chapter Thirty-Five

The crowd was at fever pitch as Blair prepared for his first opponent, stretching and getting loose.

Trev had been selected by Simon to begin Blair's fighting line up, with several others in line to go up straight after him, until Blair had been suitably dealt with.

Trev was a skilled boxer and John deemed that he and Blair were pretty evenly matched, although Trev was slightly bigger. Trev obviously fancied himself in the match up, as he had opted to step up against Blair without any weapons and had also stripped to the waist.

It was effectively a fair contest - as fair as a bare-knuckle fight that was part of a line up to the death could be anyway.

The drinks were flowing and the cocaine and speed were flying off the tables up people's noses as fast as they could be cut out into lines. The members of The Brotherhood were having the time of their lives and the night was still so young.

There was a constant noisy murmur between the gang members, as they speculated, anticipated and made bets with each other.

Then it was time to begin.

"Okay gentlemen, lady and the three cunts who are about to die. Let's get ready to rumble!" Simon announced into the microphone with gusto.

Blair stepped up, scared but masking it as best he could. He knew he had to focus and do his best to stay alive for as long as he was able. Trev was relaxed and eager to start swinging.

Simon handed the microphone to Kate.

"Okay boys, let's have a good dirty fight! Ding ding! Round one!"

Trev advanced with purpose across the ring and started throwing punches with bad intentions from the outset. Blair covered up and used his footwork to find some space for himself and literally get a foothold.

Blair came back, landing an audacious right hand lead and giving Trev something to think about.

It wasn't going to be as easy as Trev thought. He may have underestimated Blair and he would have to see by how much.

John could only sit there on his knees, watching and hoping. He and Alan exchanged glances, but there was nothing to say at this point, even with their eyes.

The situation was untenable. There was no escape for any of the three of them.

The blood was soon flowing from both men's faces and down their sweaty torsos, as they continued to lace punches into each other. Both Blair and Trev were getting tired and the punches were getting sloppier.

It was a relatively even match, but of the two of them only Blair would be forced to have another fight straight afterwards.

As Trev slammed down on his back, hard against the dance floor, it was clear he would be unable to continue. He had not been completely knocked out, but Blair had caught him with a good clean shot and put him down hard on the ground. Trev would not be able to fight on.

He was dazed as he lay there and a few fellow gang members dragged him out of the ring area and threw some water over him. Blair took the opportunity to get his breath back, as he prepared to take on the next opponent.

Simon's right-hand man, Andy, was up next and was rifling through the box of weapons. This time it did not appear that there was going to be a fair fight.

Andy was almost as sadistic as Simon and would relish the opportunity to wield one of these sickening weapons against young Blair.

Before he could select one, however, an unexpected voice boomed through the speakers.

"Fuck that! I'm gonna do this little cunt!"

It was Kate, who had picked up the microphone and announced her intent.

This was a surprise to everyone, including Simon who looked shocked and unsure that it was a good idea. Kate appeared determined though and was soon making her way down to the ring area.

Blair was raised with the attitude that you never hit a woman. Even though he was caught up in this complete nightmare, he would still rather not have to break that rule before he died.

"Hey come on guys, fair go!" he shouted out. "I don't fight with women!"

Simon laughed into the microphone, matching sniggers from among the other gang members.

"You fight with whoever I say you fight with and this woman is going to make you look like a sick faggot!"

This brought cheers from the crowd, who were keen to see this spectacle unfold. All of them were well aware of Kate's capabilities, having felt the sting of her kicks, punches, knees and elbows in the ring in the gym at Nathan House.

They all knew Blair had already made his first mistake by shouting out that he didn't want to fight a woman. She wanted to fight him and now he'd pissed her off.

Chapter Thirty-Six

Kate was making a power play of her own by putting herself forward to fight Blair next. She was effectively a woman in a man's world and was seizing this opportunity to prove herself to any remaining doubters in the gang.

Stuart often joked with her about how the gang was called The Brotherhood and she was a woman. While Stuart was only jesting, she knew there was an element of truth in what he was pointing out in banter and that some of the guys may still not have accepted her.

She hoped that after this, there would be no remaining doubt about her left in the gang.

She had dressed appropriately, in combats, trainers and a vest top. This would not have been an occasion to be caught in a skirt or dress and heels.

As she stepped into the ring, there was an audible sense of excitement and anticipation, even more so than when Trev had stepped in. The Brotherhood wanted to see this.

Kate eyed Blair from the other side of the ring. He had used the opportunity of the brief respite to get his breath back a bit, but he was still bleeding, physically exhausted and hurt.

"Seconds away, round one!" Simon announced through the microphone.

As Kate advanced towards him, Blair still did not want to do this.

"Oh fuck off guys! I'm not going to fight a fucking girl!"

He put his arms down by his sides, as if protesting the match up and refusing to fight. This gesture and these words only served to further motivate Kate, as she closed in on him ready for blood.

Blair still had his hands by his sides and was looking up at Simon for a reprieve as Kate launched a savage elbow into his face. Her right elbow connected full force with his unguarded nose, breaking it and exploding blood all over her arm and shoulder.

Her adrenaline was pumping and there would be no mercy.

Blair tried to gather himself, as blood poured out of his nose and water streamed down from his eyes. He raised his hands to protect himself from the next attack.

Kate's next onslaught came from lower down though, as she unleashed a series of fast and hard sweeping side kicks around his lower legs; left then right, left then right. Blair struggled to stay on his feet, as he stumbled back to the edge of his side of the ring.

Now he knew he was in a real fight and that Kate was a more than worthy opponent.

He had given her a head start and he was already regretting that mistake. It was time to hit a woman.

Blair stepped forward in western boxing style, in a side on stance, and started throwing quick combinations: jab, cross, jab; jab, hook, jab. Kate covered up for most of them, although a couple of punches landed and he had successfully backed her up into the centre of the ring.

She swatted away his final jab with a well timed parry and paused for a second to take stock. Now her nose was bleeding too, although the bleeding was nowhere near as bad as the bleeding from Blair's nose.

She dabbed at the blood with the extended thumb of her right hand and then licked it off, savouring the metallic taste. She then smiled at Blair in a slightly maniacal way, as she raised her hands and assumed her Thai boxing stance once again.

As the bout continued, Kate showed herself to be a savage and capable fighter. She was giving Blair a much sterner test than Trev had, even taking into account that this was his second fight in a row.

Blair was hurt, bleeding and running out of fight. Kate, on the other hand, seemed undeterred by her minor injuries and full of energy.

Blair was going down.

Kate sensed that it was time for a big finish and unleashed a fast and furious combination of punches and elbows into Blair's head as she advanced on him.

Once she was close enough, she locked her hands around his neck and threw a series of knees into his rib cage - left then right, throwing her weight into each one.

She stepped back half a step and unleashed a left elbow coming downwards and sideways into the right side of his face. This sent him collapsing to the ground.

He did what he could to protect himself, as she stamped repeatedly down on his head, until his arms were battered and tired. She had beaten the fight out of him.

Blair then lay there defeated, as Kate walked across the ring away from him and raised her arms like a champion fighter, soaking in the cheers of the crowd.

Just as the cheers reached their crescendo, she put one arm down and kept the other in the air, extending her index finger from a clenched fist.

This was to indicate that she wasn't quite finished yet.

As the crowd noise died down a little in anticipation, she took a few charging steps towards Blair. He was lying sprawled out on the dance floor and she leapt powerfully into the air above him.

She came crashing down on his unprotected face with her right knee, hitting Blair with the full force of her body, combined with the force of gravity from the leap.

There was a sickening crack that echoed through the main dance floor area and a huge amount of blood that splashed and poured from Blair's head.

His body lay there motionless in a pool of his own blood, as Kate once again stood up with her arms extended and enjoyed renewed cheers from the bloodthirsty crowd.

She had shown them exactly what she was capable of.

John looked over at Blair in despair, hoping to see some movement; some sign of life. None was forthcoming, however. He just lay there like a bloodied rag doll.

He looked dead.

NEIL WALKER

Chapter Thirty-Seven

The crowd noise remained at fever pitch, as what was left of Blair was trailed out of the ring by a couple of gang members. It still wasn't clear if he was dead or just badly injured and unconscious.

Kate took the accolades and pats on the back from her fellow members of The Brotherhood, who were now surrounding her. She was handed a glass of champagne and was offered a large line of cocaine, which she immediately snorted in one go.

She then made her way back up to the DJ booth, carrying her glass of champagne.

Soon she was beside Simon again. The queen was back beside the king.

Simon kissed her and then picked up the microphone again.

"Next up, mick number two! Johnny Boy, you have to wait and go last, coz you're our number one favourite mick!"

A couple of the gang members started cutting Alan free, while another stood a short distance away, aiming a gun at his head.

Andy once again made his way to the plastic weapons box, in preparation for facing off against his imminent opponent Alan. He had been robbed of his chance to wield one of these uniquely engineered and sickeningly brutal weapons against Blair, and was determined to make the most of his opportunity against Alan.

At first glance, Alan looked to him like a less challenging opponent than Blair. Blair had appeared to be younger and was in noticeably better shape - at least before Trev and Kate had gone to work on him.

John took the opportunity of these last few seconds, before Alan would be trailed into the ring, to pass on some valuable information to his friend.

"He's one of them. This guy you're going to fight, he's one of the four."

"You mean Lisa? One of the four that hurt Lisa?" Alan clarified.

"Yes mate. This one's all yours."

This piece of information filled Alan with a steely determination and put fire in his belly. John knew it would have this effect and he had wanted to motivate him for the challenge ahead.

He had also wanted Alan to know that he was being granted his wish; he had wanted to get his hands on one the gang members who had so viciously raped Lisa and now he would have the opportunity to do just this. He could now face off against one of the rapists and do his worst.

Alan stood up and was ushered to his side of the ring. Across from him, Andy seemed to be spoilt for choice with the selection of weapons in the plastic weapons box and was taking his time to decide.

He finally settled on an old and battered looking hockey stick that had a number of four-inch nails driven through the curved end of it. There were perhaps ten nails menacingly jutting out of the hitting end of this piece of used sports equipment.

John had played a little hockey at school, although he had preferred rugby. He had never seen a hockey stick used in this way before, however.

He had been hit on the shins enough times in his life with a hockey stick to know how much it hurt. He also knew how light and easy to wield they were and realised just how deadly this hockey stick now was, with the nails driven through the end of it.

Andy stepped into the ring, spinning the hockey stick around his hand skilfully. It was obviously not his first time handling this type of weapon, although John doubted he had specifically used a hockey stick covered in nails like this before.

Andy turned to Simon and Kate, who were looking on from the DJ booth, and held up the hockey stick. They both cheered and applauded their encouragement, as did the crowd around the ring.

Andy was obviously keen to impress Simon, as well as the rest of The Brotherhood.

Across from him, Alan was stretching and warming up for this fight. He looked more confident than Blair had and was resolved that if he going to die on this night, he was going to take this guy with him - this vile rapist.

Andy stepped up and stood squarely across from Alan, who was still stretching. Alan was not going to waste a single second of his warm up time; plus he felt that calmly stretching like this made him seem more relaxed and intimidating to his adversary.

"Okay Andy, you're up! Skewer this fucking pig!" shouted Simon into the microphone.

This heralded the commencement of a seemingly very uneven contest.

Andy stepped forward cautiously into the middle of the ring, swinging his hockey stick in front of him like he was trying to create a barrier to attack. He was hoping to hurt Alan and not get hurt himself.

Alan began bouncing around the edge of the ring like Muhammad Ali, obviously viewing this as a better strategy in the situation than a more rigid, head on stance. Andy turned like the hand of a clock, swinging his hockey stick, as Alan danced around him on his tiptoes.

Andy soon realised that he couldn't continue like this or he would end up looking scared and foolish. After all, he had a weapon and should have nothing to fear from an unarmed man.

He picked his moment and charged forward at Alan, swinging his hockey stick across and downwards, as he wielded it from above.

Alan managed to mostly avoid the blow, ducking down and sideways to escape it. Andy did catch him a little, however, scraping the jagged nails across the top of his ducked down head, raking them through his hair.

Alan stood up and danced around again, this time claiming the middle of the ring. Andy was realising that there was a chance this wasn't going to be as straightforward as he had first thought.

He had hoped he would just have to carry his weapon into the ring, attack Alan with it and beat him to death as violently as he could with it, without much fight back.

Andy was not a courageous warrior or a brave fighter; he was a sadistic coward who wanted to use violence and present himself as strong, but only when he felt the dynamics of the situation meant that he was unlikely to be hurt himself.

As the fight continued, Alan was getting the nails raked across his flesh and had blood pouring from cuts on his head and torso. He had also managed to land a few punches on Andy though, counterpunching on the retreat from the cutting hockey stick swings.

Blood was dripping from the nails on the hockey stick and the crowd was going crazy. Using an unusual and cruelly brutal weapon like this had upped the ante for them in the entertainment department and the gang was absolutely loving it.

As the members of The Brotherhood looked on at this incredible, violent spectacle, they roared and shouted enthusiastically. They were sipping alcoholic drinks, as well as snorting cocaine and speed.

Alan was bleeding and hurt, but not beaten. He was still determined to see this guy dead.

Having fought with Andy and his hockey stick for long enough to be able to predict his attacks to an extent, he had devised a strategy to take him down that he thought might work.

John watched on, frustrated that he couldn't help his lifelong friend and itching to get his hands and legs free and charge into the thick of it.

John knew he couldn't help Alan, but he also knew how capable he was and he still hoped his friend could pull something out of the bag and punish this guy.

As Andy advanced, swinging the hockey stick hard towards the left side of his head, Alan saw his chance and put his plan into action. With split second timing, as the sharp end of the modified hockey stick closed in on his face, he threw up his left arm to take the blow and allowed the nails to sink into his flesh, so that it became stuck in his arm.

He then dragged it downwards with his arm and pulled it out of Andy's grip.

As Andy lurched forward to try to recover his weapon, Alan leant his weight down low to his right and flew up at Andy's face with a perfectly aimed right uppercut.

His fist landed with pinpoint accuracy and maximum force on the tip of Andy's nose, driving his nasal bone unstoppably upwards into his brain. There was a burst of blood, as Andy's nose seemed to almost disappear into his head, changing the shape and look of his face instantly and significantly.

Andy dropped down with a thud, landing on his knees with all his weight. There was blood pouring from what was left of his nose, his lifeless eyes staring into nothingness.

He was dead before he hit the ground, as he collapsed forward on to his disfigured face.

"Fuck you!" Alan shouted aggressively, pointing down at his vanquished and deceased opponent.

The noisy crowd was instantly silenced and in shock. This had not been part of Simon's party plan.

Alan took the opportunity of those moments, during which the crowd was stunned, to hold his arms up in the air, like a boxing champion who had just won a world title.

This incensed Simon and the rest of The Brotherhood.

"Mob that cunt! Hit him with everything!" Simon angrily spat into the microphone.

Around ten of the gang members - the ones who were quickest off the blocks - converged on Alan, swinging punches. A few others hastily made for the weapons box and grabbed the first weapons that came to hand, before joining the angry attack mob.

Alan had enjoyed his moment of glory, his time in the sun. Now he was going to have to pay for it.

John could only see it from the outside of the circle of blows that surrounded Alan. Among the weapons savagely beating his friend, he noted a particularly nasty looking baseball bat with razor blades driven into it, as well as a cricket bat wrapped in barbed wire.

These modified bats and other weapons, along with the fists, elbows and shoes of the other attackers, were all soon red with blood. They were attacking Alan like sharks in a feeding frenzy.

John felt a wave of guilt now, as well as an overwhelming urge to help Alan. There was nothing he could do though.

He just sat there, bound on his knees, watching this mob of vicious gang members tear his friend apart.

Chapter Thirty-Eight

John still wasn't sure if Blair was alive or dead, but as the mob around Alan eventually stepped back, there could be no doubt about his status.

He didn't even look like a dead body; more like chunks of butchers' meat in a lake of blood. They had killed him, in a depraved and savage way.

"Oh yes!" Simon shouted gleefully into the microphone, as he got a good look at what they had done to Alan.

As John looked up at the DJ booth, he could see that Simon and Kate were very pleased with the outcome. Simon had still lost his best friend in The Brotherhood, however.

And as for Alan, he had gone out swinging, just as he would have wanted. Plus, he had managed to take one of Lisa's rapists with him.

In a way, this had been his final wish and he had made it come true before he died.

John was devastated by what had happened to his friends, as Simon had no doubt planned and intended. He vowed to go out the same way as Alan had though, fearlessly fighting whoever was put in front of him.

"That cunt is looking like chopped liver down there. Looking at that is making me hungry," Simon taunted John through the speakers.

He then gave instruction to his crowd of gang members.

"Seriously, can we get that mess cleaned up boys? I don't want Johnny Boy slipping over while he's getting beaten to death."

A handful of the Brotherhood members acted quickly and started mopping up the blood and bagging up the chunks of flesh and body parts into strong black refuse bags.

This was no doubt a sign of things to come, thought John. Soon they would all be tidied into bags and buried in the ground, never to be found.

As the clean up came to a conclusion, John looked up at the DJ booth again to see that Dave had joined Simon and Kate up there.

Dave appeared to be negotiating with Simon. John reasoned that Big, Bad, Black Dave was staking a claim to have first crack at him in the ring.

This was fine with John, who would be extremely glad to get his hands on another one of the gang members who had staged the Sydney attack; another one of the rapists who had defiled his girlfriend.

Dave seemed to get the answer he wanted and made his way down to the dance floor again.

Simon signalled the guys nearest to John to untie him and two of them did so, while a third kept a gun on him at all times. If they had been careful with the other two, they knew they needed to be extra careful with John.

John stood up and could see Dave stripping to the waist, just outside the circle of gang members and tables that made up the makeshift boxing ring.

The murmur of pre-fight chatter and the consumption of drugs and alcohol were now well under way again. They had seemingly got over the loss of their 'brother' at this point and were ready once again to be entertained.

John planned to oblige them.

He was pleased to see Dave stripping to the waist and believed that his taking his t-shirt off signalled that he probably wanted to have a fair, stand up fight, in the same way that Trev had against Blair.

Dave was a very skilled fighter and a cocky person, so he probably wanted to seize the chance to prove himself and show off in front of his fellow gang members.

Dave was both a well-trained boxer and an experienced and well-practiced kickboxer. He had dabbled in other martial arts as well.

Dave would provide as tough a test as any one individual in this group could give John. Far from being nervous about it, however, John was relishing it.

As the two fighters faced off against each other from their opposing sides of the ring, Simon once again served as house announcer.

"Okay boys, it's time for the main event! Finalise your bets, take a big fucking line of coke or speed and watch our number one enemy get fucking minced!"

The crowd went wild - cheering, clapping and even jumping around like an energetic football crowd. They then swiftly began following Simon's instructions regarding gambling and the consumption of narcotics.

They finished sorting out their bets and there was a flurry of snorting, as they all made well and truly sure that their cocaine and speed buzz was topped up, before this incredibly exciting spectacle began.

Once Simon was satisfied that everyone - including the two fighters - was ready, he handed the microphone to Kate, who was still standing in her position beside him as queen of The Brotherhood.

"Okay guys, the one you've all been waiting for! No way this fucker gets out alive! It's time for John Kennedy versus The Brotherhood!"

Chapter Thirty-Nine

This was it.

John Kennedy had watched two of his closest friends horrifically beaten, right in front of him, by multiple opponents from the membership of The Brotherhood. Alan had been literally torn to pieces and Blair looked to have been beaten to death. Now it was his turn.

If Alan and Blair had been the support acts of this horrendous event of sadistic entertainment, then John was the headliner.

At this point, John knew things looked hopeless and that there appeared to be no conceivable way he could make it out of the ring alive. He was there to die.

He remembered his own resolution in this moment, however; the one he had stated aloud to Blair and Peter in Vincenzo's nightclub on their last night in Belfast, before they had left for Manchester.

As they had sat there together, drinking and taking drugs, John had vowed that there would be no more holding back on his part, mentally or physically. He had meant it too.

Now it didn't seem that there was much he could do with his intelligence to mentally think himself out of this situation, although he would remain alert to any opportunities while he still had breath in his lungs and thoughts in his head.

Physically though, he could still use everything he had against any and every opponent presented to him. He would hold nothing back and show absolutely no quarter.

Just what could he do with his body after all these years of training? If he was going to die on this night and in this place, how many members of The Brotherhood could he take with him?

It was time to find out, as Kate finished giving her pre-combat speech into the microphone and John prepared for bare-knuckle war.

"Triple B, take him down!" Kate shouted through the PA.

The crowd erupted again and now resembled the mosh pit at the front of a heavy metal concert. They were at absolute fever pitch, as the two fighters moved towards each other in the centre of the ring.

As he closed in on John, Dave took the opportunity to milk his moment in the sun. He raised his arm in the air and shouted, "Triple B!"

The mob went crazy for this and began to loudly chant, "Triple B! Triple B! Triple B!"

Adrenaline surged through Dave as he threw his first punch at John, a quick snapping jab with his left fist. John parried it perfectly and moved to his left, before Dave could follow up with a right cross.

Dave turned and advanced again, this time leading with a left hook, which John bobbed under. He snapped a right hook into the exposed left side of Dave's face and moved right.

Dave was angry now, as John took position in the centre of the ring. He was still confident and he had known all along that this was not going to be easy.

When John had been in The Brotherhood, Dave had heard all the stories of John's fighting prowess and had seen a few examples of him in action in nightclub battles and on the streets.

But when he would watch him train or occasionally spar with him, he couldn't help but fancy himself against him. He had believed John to be overrated and no match for him. Was there any chance that he had he been wrong?

The two continued their skilled and nuanced match up, as Simon and Kate looked on with a perfect view of the action. Simon had not planned to allow anyone to have a one on one fight with John, let alone without weapons.

This was to be a spectacle in punishment - an absolute and total victory. Dave had persuaded Simon that he could handle it and beat John, however.

His eagerness to impress had pleased Simon, who was enjoying his new role as the king of The Brotherhood. Perhaps this had influenced and clouded his decision.

Kate had heard a lot about John Kennedy and was impressed by what she now saw against Big, Bad, Black Dave. She still would have loved to get into the ring with John herself and test herself against him, but she knew it wasn't the pragmatic move and that Simon would have rightly vetoed the idea.

Both Dave and John were landing good shots on each other, but John was taking pleasure in making Dave miss and taunting him, sticking his chin out with his hands down and goading him.

He was trying to make Dave completely lose his temper and his composure, and it was starting to work.

John parried away a right cross in a way that seemed almost as if he had swatted it away from him with ease, like a cat lazily swatting a fly. With this, Dave promptly lost it.

He came after John with wild swings and big overhand rights. He was playing right into John's hands and it looked like his control had gone out the window. His technique was slipping, as his emotions got the better of him.

A particularly telegraphed overhand right came flying with a lot of force straight at John's face. With his fast reflexes and inch-perfect timing, he felt like he had all the time in the world to react.

He slipped the punch and it went flying past his head, as he shifted his weight on to his left foot and came flying back at Dave with a powerful left hook. It landed right on the side of his jawbone and sent him lurching to his left, dazed by the blow.

John followed up swiftly with a fast combination of powerful punches; a left jab, a right hook, and a left hook.

Then, as Dave was stumbling backwards, came what seemed like the coup de grace. He delivered an expertly guided and executed right uppercut.

The uppercut connected forcefully with the point of Dave's chin. It landed with over one and a half pounds of pressure, jarring his brain and rendering him unconscious. At this point, it looked like it was all over, as Dave fell backwards.

John moved forward swiftly, however, following his falling motion.

He caught his throat powerfully with a finger grip from his right hand. He then grabbed the back of his neck with his left hand, to stop gravity pulling him out of his grasp.

John now had him by the throat, with his fingers jabbing through the flesh around his windpipe.

Dave's whole body weight was pulling downwards and John had his fingers bored right into his throat, in the area around his windpipe. As he removed his left hand from the back of his neck, gravity was working for him and against his unconscious opponent.

As Dave's weight pulled his flaccid, horizontal body to the floor, John wrenched his right hand upwards, tearing out his windpipe with an eruption of blood.

He then held the bloody body part in the air above his head. The blood was running down his outstretched arm, while Dave's dead body lay motionless on the floor.

John felt elated to have exacted such bloody vengeance on another one of the guys who had raped Lisa. This is what he had wanted all along - to get his hands on these guys and hurt them mercilessly.

As the angry mob bayed for blood and looked to Simon for instruction, he felt sure that this was the end and they would now kill him without further delay.

Chapter Forty

John knew he would not have much time, as he held the disembodied windpipe aloft in the air. He took his chance in the few seconds he had and angrily threw Dave's windpipe up at Simon and Kate in the DJ booth.

Simon instinctively ducked sideways out of the way of the well-aimed flying body part and managed to just avoid it. Kate was not so lucky and it hit her, full force, on the side of the face.

It then dropped to the floor beneath her, leaving a bloody mark on her cheek.

Far from being shocked and angry though, she smiled and dabbed the blood with her thumb, before putting it to her mouth and licking it. If she had been unnerved by this turn of events, she hid it well.

Simon was even further infuriated, however, and screamed out to the gang, not even taking the time to pick up and use the microphone.

"Grab that cunt! Get him, but don't fucking kill him!"

The makeshift ring made up of members of The Brotherhood immediately closed in on John.

They dragged him to the ground, punching, kicking and stomping him. He tried to cover up as best he could, but he could feel the blows cracking into him all over his head and body.

Simon and Kate sped down from the DJ booth to get hands-on with the matter at hand.

"Right, that's enough!" Simon announced.

He had to keep control of the situation and the members of The Brotherhood.

"Put him on his front and hold him down."

The crowd stepped back, giving the five or six gang members who kept hold of John room to turn him over on to his front. There were too many of them and he was too beaten up and weakened to resist much or fight back.

Once he was face down on the dance floor, a few of them sat on his torso and legs, keeping him in place.

"Hold out his fucking arms," Simon then instructed.

His orders were obeyed and John was soon flat on his front, with his arms stretched out in front of him and to the side. Simon reached something out of his pocket and knelt down beside John's head to talk to him.

He held out the object, putting it right up close to John's face. It was the Swiss Army knife with Sydney embossed on it.

"Remember these tasteful Aussie souvenirs? I bought this off your bitch in her shop in Sydney. Yes, as I recall it was just before me and the boys spent the whole day breaking her in for you."

"Fuck you!" John shouted out from beneath the bodies weighing down on him.

It was a struggle to get the words out, but he couldn't help but shout them.

"This little thing came in handy for keeping her entertained," he taunted.

He then unfurled the corkscrew from the Swiss Army knife.

"This was her favourite; we had hours of fun with this bad boy. Let's see how you like it Johnny Boy."

Simon then stood up, holding the Swiss army knife - with the corkscrew sticking out from it - up for the rest of The Brotherhood to see.

"This is what happens when you fuck with The Brotherhood. We fuck with you and take no prisoners. This cunt isn't going to get the mercy of just getting beaten to death; we're going to make sure he goes out screaming!"

This brought a cheer from the cocaine, speed and alcohol fuelled crowd, who had become a little subdued after Dave had been killed.

"He used his right hand to kill our brother, so we start with his right hand!"

Another cheer went up as Simon looked down on the situation at his feet, thinking of what needed to be done logistically so he could get to work.

"Right, a couple of you stamp on his hand till it's sitting open, flat on the ground. I can't work with a clenched fist."

A couple of gang members enthusiastically stepped forward to stomp on John's hand, but so did Kate.

"Do you mind if I have the pleasure?" she asked in a flirtatious tone.

The two gang members that had stepped forward looked at each other and one of them nodded out, leaving the other one to get to work with Kate.

Both Kate and the remaining gang member savagely stamped down on John's clenched right hand, being careful not to stomp on each other's feet.

John could only hold out for so long and eventually opened his hand out flat. Kate then stood on his outstretched fingers, pushing all her weight down on them, to ensure he couldn't clench his fist again.

"I've got him babe," Kate reassured Simon. "Do your worst."

This is precisely what Simon planned to do. He knelt down once again, so that he could lean forward over John's right hand.

He then positioned the Swiss Army knife in his hand so that the corkscrew was poking out between his index and middle finger.

He lined the corkscrew up with the middle of the back of John's right hand and pressed as much weight down on it as he could. With all the force he could muster, he slowly twisted it, so that it drilled, bit by bit, down into John's hand.

John had no choice but to scream in pain, as it went in deeper and deeper.

It didn't take long before Simon felt the corkscrew hitting the hard surface of the dance floor beneath John's right hand. He had managed to get it all the way through.

Now that he had accomplished his goal, he wanted to add insult to injury.

Instead of screwing it back out again, he pressed his right foot down on John's wrist, while still kneeling down on his left knee, ready to spring up. Kate was still holding his hand firmly in place with her foot on his fingers.

Simon forcefully yanked the corkscrew out of John's hand, while pushing upwards with his legs, tearing the curling metal corkscrew through John's flesh and out in a single, agonising move.

Simon held the bloody instrument in the air, heralding a rapturous ovation from the bloodthirsty mob of Brotherhood members.

The king was back in control of proceedings.

"Glad you enjoyed that boys!" he bellowed at the crowd, so that it echoed through the large main area of the nightclub. "But that was just the warm up!"

A large cheer went up through the crowd, who were once more in full voice.

"That was the starter and now it's time for the main course! We're going to kill this cunt! But before he dies, we're going to make him wish he was fucking dead!"

Chapter Forty-One

"Flip him on to his back and hold him down again," Simon commanded.

He walked away purposefully in the direction of the DJ booth. He then disappeared into some sort of storage room in behind the main nightclub area, while another three gang members joined in with the ones who had been sitting on John and flipped him on to his back.

Again, there were too many of them and John was too weakened and hurt to struggle.

John was feeling like tenderised meat at this point. He was now spread-eagled on his back, with his limbs being held out firmly.

As he looked up, he could see Kate just staring down at him and smiling. And she wasn't smiling at him in a sympathetic way; she was smiling at him and relishing the scenario. She appeared to be enjoying what was happening to him and looking forward to what was about to happen next.

Simon clearly had a plan B in place for just this kind of turn of events. If John fought too well, or hurt a member of The Brotherhood too badly, Simon was hardly going to allow him to continue hacking his way through his troops.

John had proved himself to be just as dangerous as his reputation and Simon was going to take no more chances with him.

Plus, to gruesomely dispatch John himself would only add to his status as the leader of the gang. He would further cement his place as their king and forever be known as the man who killed John Kennedy.

In his time away from the gang, John's reputation had only grown among them. He had become a kind of Bogeyman; he was viewed in a way that was almost bigger than life, as well as being utterly despised.

John Kennedy was seen as the exception that proved the rule; you must stay loyal to The Brotherhood and your fellow gang members at all costs and no matter what happens.

Simon re-entered the main part of the nightclub and John was doing his best to tip his head forwards, to see what he had gone to get and get an idea of what was coming.

As soon as John saw what he was carrying, he knew exactly what Simon had in store for him and he was now genuinely terrified.

It took him back, in his own mind, to one of his most haunting memories from his time in The Brotherhood. The time they took a rival gang hostage, in the Moss Side area of Manchester, and tortured one of them for information.

John had played his part in it; there was no denying that. It certainly had not been his idea, however, and he had been the last to know the details.

Doug and Sanjay - and possibly Simon - had been the ones who conceived and planned the cruel and macabre interrogation method.

As Simon re-emerged, his hands full of hateful pain to come, John was reminded of Gordon. Gordon was the name of the gang member they tortured and killed that night; John would never forget it.

In his left hand, Simon was carrying a black plastic bucket, with the sharp end of a circular saw peering out of the top of it.

In his right hand were four pairs of plastic safety goggles, obviously for use with the circular saw.

He would never forget his own feeling of shock and horror when he had watched Sanjay carry the very same items into that kitchen of the house in Moss Side. The realisation of the brutality they were about to unleash.

Now that brutality was about to be unleashed on him.

Simon placed the bucket containing the circular saw and the four pairs of goggles on the floor, directly beside Kate. Then he walked back towards the storage room area, without saying anything or shouting to the crowd - as if what he had just brought into the room did not deserve a mention - just as Sanjay had done when he brought the same things into the house in Moss Side.

Simon quickly returned from the storage room, this time carrying a pile of medical gowns and rubber gloves. He dropped them on the ground beside the goggles, bucket and saw.

It was once again time for him to address the crowd.

"Okay, who wants to help me end this piece of shit?"

There was a clamour of raised hands and shouts, as everyone seemed to want to volunteer.

"Okay, I'll leave it up to my beautiful assistant," he said, gesturing in Kate's direction.

"No problem Simon. How many helpers do you need?"

"Three. Or two, if you want to help."

"Two then," Kate responded to Simon, as he knew she would.

There was no way she was going to miss her chance to be part of this. The way she saw it, this would be talked about for years to come in The Brotherhood and she wanted to be involved in it.

"Okay, you and you," she said quickly, pointing at the first two gang members who caught her eye.

She didn't want to be seen to contemplate her decision or to be selecting her favourites. That may have led to resentment in future and detracted from the positive impact this was going to have on her reputation in the soon to be expanding gang.

Simon lifted up the four pairs of goggles from the floor, handing two of them to the two selected volunteers, giving one to Kate and keeping one for himself.

He then picked up the gowns and gloves, handing a gown and a pair of gloves to each of the other three soon-to-be butchers, retaining a gown and a pair of gloves for his own use.

"Hey, while we're getting ready, someone go and stick some fucking music back on. Something fucked up please!" Simon declared, in an open request to the group, as he began getting into his gown.

This brought an enthusiastic murmur from the ranks of The Brotherhood, followed by a slight surge of a handful of them towards the DJ booth.

Wanting to ensure there was no lull in the mood and no one felt that they were just waiting around or weren't involved, Simon gave out further instructions to the group.

"The rest of you, get the biggest line of coke and speed you've ever had in your lives and put it straight up your fucking nose! I mean cut the two together and get the big super lines right up you! You're going to want to be buzzing for this!"

This brought another cheer and seemed to re-invigorate the crowd, who rushed to the little tables they had been using for drinks, cocaine and speed. They began folding cocaine and speed together with credit cards and cutting out monstrous lines of this combination super drug.

"Make sure you have a line ready for the boys who are holding him down as well," he added.

This brought smiles to the faces of the guys who were holding John in place on the ground.

As Simon, Kate and the two selected volunteers got ready for the amateur medical procedure they were about to participate in, three gang members were frantically looking through records and CDs in the DJ booth. They were debating what the perfect soundtrack for this historic moment would be.

Apart from the guys still holding John down, the rest of them were cutting, snorting and drinking with enthusiastic gusto.

The bloodthirsty mob were buzzing on a cocktail of cocaine, speed, alcohol and adrenaline, as Simon, Kate and the two selected gang members finally got their gowns, goggles and gloves on.

"Okay, gather round again! Stay a couple of feet back though. I've done this before and you'll want to leave a splash zone."

This brought laughter and cheers from the mob, as they took their positions in a semi-circle around the spread-eagled John. Simon lifted the circular saw up from out of the plastic bucket and looked up to the DJ booth.

"Well lads, get the fucking tune on and get down here for the show!"

As they started the music playing, it was clear that all three of them were happy with their choice of tune. They all scurried down, as the atmospheric start of the track began to ring out through the speakers.

They quickly snorted a large line of cocaine and speed mix and joined the rest of The Brotherhood in the semi-circle around John.

John recognised the song straight away: 'Open Up' by Leftfield. He wasn't sure if they had just selected it as an excellent, banging, fucked up tune, or because they found the track title and lyrics appropriate and amusing, given what was about to happen.

The humorous aspect of the title of this chosen track was not lost on John; 'Open Up'. While he himself didn't find it funny under the circumstances, it was admittedly apt. After all, they were about to open him up.

NEIL WALKER

Chapter Forty-Two

In the house in Moss Side, Gordon could have avoided being dismembered with the circular saw or stopped it at any time; all he had to do was talk.

John had marvelled at the time, and ever since, at the fact that he didn't. Gordon held out and took the pain. Now, John would have no choice but to do the same.

The Leftfield tune 'Open Up' had moved into the main, pounding, upbeat part of the track and an energetic, bouncing crowd were gathered round his spread-eagled, shirtless body, as he attempted in vain to struggle against those holding him in place.

The buzzing, drug eyed mob surrounding him were baying for blood and savagery.

The duty of pinning John down on the dance floor had shifted from the original group, to a gowned and goggled Kate and the two gowned and goggled gang members she had quickly selected from those who had volunteered. They were all forcing their weight down on the middle of his body, while holding his arms and legs outstretched, ready for the circular saw about to be wielded by Simon.

John's field of vision wasn't great in this moment, but from among those he could see, Peter caught his eye; the guy he had thought was one of his best friends, as well as a trusted colleague in the drug world.

He had been extremely shocked by the revelation that Peter had betrayed him and secretly been working as part of The Brotherhood.

Given the number of shocking and horrific events that had unfolded before him in such a short period of time, he hadn't really had time to fully process this betrayal and the fact that he had completely misjudged Peter and clearly hadn't really known who he was.

He had let Peter into his mother's house; let him eat Christmas dinner with him and his family. Peter had even tried and enjoyed his grandfather's stew - letting him in to an exclusive club, only usually made up of family members and their very closest friends.

Now, Peter was looking down on him, full of cocaine, speed and alcohol. He appeared to have the same eager look on his face as the rest of The Brotherhood, but for them John was public enemy number one.

Could Peter really have hated him that much? Did he really want to see him chopped into pieces with a circular saw and watch him bleed to death in front of him?

Maybe he did, or perhaps he was just doing exactly what John had done when he was in The Brotherhood; putting on a front and showing them exactly what they needed to see to make them think he was just the same as them.

Either way, it didn't matter now; Peter was the enemy and so was everyone else around him and on top of him.

He braced himself for an unbearably painful and gruesome death, as The Brotherhood had the time of their lives exacting their terrible revenge on him.

A smiling and gleeful Simon pulled his goggles over his eyes and leaned over John with the circular saw - which was not yet turned on - taunting him.

He touched the blade against his left leg, to indicate that's the limb he would start with, not that it really mattered when he planned to cut off all of his limbs anyway.

Simon stood back up, looking down on John, still smiling and banging his head a little in time with the music. He was fully enjoying the climax of his New Year's Eve party spectacular.

With that, Simon switched on the circular saw and the blade began furiously spinning, further bringing home to John just how horrific and grisly his death was going to be. John closed his eyes and prepared for the end.

He had always prided himself on never being afraid and had often joked that he laughed in the face of death. Now that the end was upon him though, he was scared. He feared the pain and he feared the end.

John was not a religious man, so for him this really was the end. The pieces of him that remained would be buried along with the hacked up remains of his friend Alan, the members of the Brotherhood who had not managed to survive, and probably the body of his friend Blair as well.

If Kate hadn't killed Blair in the ring, John felt sure they'd either murder what was left of him or just throw him in the mass grave and bury him alive.

He mentally prepared for death in the few seconds he had left, doing his best to block out the incredibly loud music, the buzzing of the circular saw and noise of the baying crowd.

He pictured Lisa, smiling and lying beside him in bed. He pictured holding her as they laughed together. After everything that he'd been through, that was what really mattered; that was all he cared about.

This was it; an end that's just in sight.

He focused on the soothing, loving image of himself with Lisa, imagining her touch, and prepared to let go of his life.

NEIL WALKER

Chapter Forty-Three

As John drifted in his mind to the place where he was happiest, he was drawn back into the world of violence and drug gangs with a bang - literally with a bang.

A gunshot rang out loudly through the main dance floor area of The Casa, so loud that it could be heard over the thumping music, crowd noise and the sound of the circular saw.

John opened his eyes to see a second shot explode off the blade mechanism of the circular saw, sending sparks flying off it and causing the spinning blade to fail.

Simon looked up in the direction of the balcony area, to see where the shots had come from, before dropping the circular saw at his feet and running in the opposite direction. He was quickly followed by Kate, who leapt off John like a pouncing cheetah and sprinted away in the same direction.

Then all hell broke loose in The Casa, with gunshots echoing around the main part of the nightclub, as the energetic sounds of Leftfield continued to bang out through the speakers.

The two gowned and goggled gang members, who had also been holding John down, jumped off him and he was able to look behind him and see what was going on.

The Brotherhood members were scattered throughout the nightclub and pulling out their guns. They were already under a barrage of gunfire and some were dropping before they could even draw and fire their weapons.

John had been dazed, weakened and ready for death. Now adrenaline flooded his body and he leapt to his feet, ready and eager for action.

Straight away he grabbed one of the gowned gang members from behind by the throat. This gang member had already wrenched off his goggles, so he could properly see the targets he was shooting at. He had barely fired a single shot before John had his hands on him though.

John powered the heel of his right foot into the back of the guy's right knee and slammed him to the ground by his neck. He then released the grip he had on his throat, only to pound a devastating right elbow into his face, knocking him unconscious.

As he took the guy's gun from his limp hand and once again stood up, any lingering thoughts about restraint or any kind of mercy were long gone.

He fired a single shot down into the guy's head - right between his eyes - and spun around to face the intense gun battle that was unfolding.

The large number of gun-wielding men, firing freely down on The Brotherhood from the balcony that surrounded the main area of the nightclub, all seemed to be Asian and John quickly saw a couple of familiar faces; Ali and Raheem.

Ali's gang had arrived mob-handed and well armed, and they were unleashing a furious hail of bullets on the members of The Brotherhood.

If he'd had time to feel guilty about jumping to the conclusion that Ali had betrayed him, maybe John would have. As it was, there was no time for anything other than the single purpose of the present moment.

John raised his gun and began running towards the side of the main nightclub area where the toilets were. While bolting across the dance floor, he kept his head turned and his eyes fixed on the crowd, firing off a steady stream of carefully aimed shots.

His bullets impacted on the backs of at least three Brotherhood members, as he raced for cover, gun blazing.

When he got to the side of the dance floor, he ducked down on his knees beside the still slumped and lifeless body of his friend Blair.

He fired off a couple more shots and then looked down at his friend for signs of life. There were none, so John took his pulse by placing the fingers of his left hand on the appropriate spot on Blair's neck, while still holding the gun in his right.

His right hand had been agonisingly injured by the corkscrew of Simon's Swiss Army knife, but the pain and discomfort were now gone. This was no longer his hurt and injured hand; this was his gun hand.

Of course, he could fire a gun to a pretty high standard with his left hand as well, but in this moment his left hand was urgently needed to check for Blair's pulse.

John was filled with a sense of relief when he found it. Blair still had a pulse; he was alive. He had been badly hurt, but not killed.

As he knelt over his friend - a relieved man - Ali and Raheem arrived beside him, having come down the stairs and run the gauntlet along the side of the main nightclub area.

"You okay?" Ali shouted at him, over the almost deafening noise of loud dance music mixed with the barrage of gunfire.

"Yeah!" John shouted back.

He took his left hand off Blair's neck and used it to give a thumbs up signal.

John was hurt, bleeding and his still naked upper body was covered in blood and painful injuries. At this point, he was more adrenaline than man, however, and for the purposes of what needed to happen now he was okay.

Raheem and Ali fired their pistols from a kneeling position beside John and the unconscious Blair. John immediately joined in. The Brotherhood members were dropping like flies in bursts of blood around The Casa.

Ali turned back to face John to issue another shouted question.

"What's the plan now?"

John answered instantly, needing no time to think about his response.

"Kill them all!"

NEIL WALKER

Chapter Forty-Four

John and Ali didn't speak, as they drove through the blackened night of the English countryside in Alan's car. There was no need for them to exchange words at this stage, as they knew exactly what they were going to do.

John was in no mood for conversation anyway, only for action. This night was not over by a long way, as far as he was concerned.

As the chaos of the gun battle had raged in The Casa, Ali and his gang had done their best to follow John's instruction and kill them all.

They had been in a closed off nightclub in the middle of an otherwise deserted part of the city on New Year's Eve, with loud, banging dance music blaring from within, so they had very little fear of discovery by law enforcement as the blood and bullets had rained down in The Casa.

And there had been no need to worry about reinforcements arriving from The Brotherhood; the members of the gang had been virtually all there, as the iconic rave venue became a shooting gallery.

Almost every known member of The Brotherhood had been inside The Casa, facing the hail of bullets. Amid the carnage, however, Simon and Kate had escaped.

Ali and John weren't sure how many other members of The Brotherhood had gone with them, if any. There had been no time to take stock before they had rushed to the car and sped off in pursuit of the king and queen of The Brotherhood. They were almost positive about where the escapees would be heading.

When you understand the nature of a thing, you know exactly what it is capable of.

While it wasn't the most logical step to go to Nathan House, John felt sure Simon would want to collect whatever money, drugs and weapons he had there, before attempting to disappear.

Simon would have been unperturbed by the deaths of his so-called brothers, but would be concerned about the loss of power, money and freedom of opportunity. He was a selfish, cold-blooded man and he appeared to have found a like-minded partner in Kate.

How the two of them had found each other, or indeed how the pair of them had ended up being as sick and twisted as they both clearly were, John did not know.

What John did know was that they would most likely be speeding back to Nathan House and he just hoped that he and Ali could get there in time.

Ali was driving; John may well have handled this part on his own, but he still hadn't had a chance to learn to drive. Like many before him, Ali had found this hard to believe. There were more pressing concerns at hand though, than John's inability to drive an automobile.

Ali and his gang had really come through for him. They had arrived and broken into The Casa just in the nick of time.

John was well aware that Ali had saved his life and would be grateful to him for his actions forever, if they could both survive the night. He would make sure that he kept his promises to his new comrade in arms.

Even Raheem - who had been seething with hate towards him and eager to chop off his hands only a few days previously - had come through for him and come good. He had volunteered to help Blair and make sure he got the kind of medical attention that wouldn't alert the authorities.

The rest of Ali's gang had been left in The Casa, tasked with clean up duty. There was a lot of blood and mess to clean up and a lot of bodies to dispose of.

This was not their first rodeo, however, and they knew what they were doing.

No member of The Brotherhood who had been trapped in The Casa would be left alive, and all of their bodies - and indeed all traces of them - would be cleared away, as if nothing had ever happened.

The only thing that the police could realistically have been called to deal with was the violence at The Doom Room, and both John and Ali seriously doubted that the staff in The Doom Room would call the police. To operate the way it did, The Doom Room was a nightclub that needed to stay well and truly off police radar.

Some of Ali's gang would need discreet medical treatment as well, as the gunfight had not been entirely one-sided. The element of surprise and the intensity of the opening exchange led by Ali's guys meant that most of the casualties were on The Brotherhood's side though, and it didn't seem like Ali's gang would suffer any fatalities.

Ali had got a t-shirt for John to wear from one of his guys, as John wasn't sure what The Brotherhood members had done with his and there was no time to look for it. They had also found a medical kit behind the bar at The Casa to treat and bandage John's hand as best they could, considering the hurry they had been in.

John was still running on a ridiculous amount of adrenaline and injuries and pain were concerns for another time.

The car slowed as they approached the tall black metal gates, which were very familiar to John, even in the darkness. Usually you needed to use a remote control to open them electronically, but they had been left lying wide open.

John wasn't sure if this meant that Simon and Kate had been and gone already, or if they had just hurried into the house, with a view to speeding back out through the open gates as quickly as possible, once they had collected what they wanted.

The small gold plaque attached high on one of the gates announcing that they were entering 'Nathan House' was visible, as the light from the car glinted off it.

As they rolled up the driveway, Ali couldn't fail to notice the size of the grounds contained around the main building, even in the dark of the night. They were huge, with grass and greenery stretching back for what seemed like miles.

As they pulled up at the building itself, Ali marvelled at what he could only have described as a mansion.

"Nice fucking gaff mate," he commented to John.

John had long since lost any wonder or awe for the magnificent house and grounds.

"Let's do this," was all John had to say, before the pair of them got out of the car.

The lights were on in Nathan House, but again, this could either have meant that Simon and Kate had already left in a hurry and were in fact already gone, or that they were still there, making swift preparations to flee the scene with all they could carry.

Anyone in there would have seen them pull up by now and it was important to act fast, in the hope that Simon and Kate had not had enough time to get in and out of the house and make their getaway.

"Keys," was John's quick request to Ali.

He threw them to him over the top of the car.

John hurried to the boot and opened it. He grabbed the weapons bag and from underneath it he also lifted out two black bulletproof vests.

"Here, take one of these," John said to Ali, holding out the bulletproof vests.

Ali arrogantly replied, "I've always got a gun, but I never wear a vest."

John wasn't sure if this was bravado or a half joke, with Ali always having intended to put one on. He was determined that he would make him wear one though, regardless.

"Fuck off and put it on," he decreed.

Ali made no further protests or comments - taking one of the bulletproof vests and putting it on over his t-shirt - indicating that he had indeed always been planning to take one.

"You need a gun?"

Ali smiled and pulled up his t-shirt, revealing that he had two pistols tucked into his trousers.

"Okay then, let's get down to business."

They made their way up to the main doors in their bulletproof vests, John carrying the weapons bag in his left hand and holding a .45 automatic he had taken from it in his right. Ali had taken out one of the pistols that had been tucked into his trousers and was holding it in a standard two-handed grip.

The two of them were ready for war and they hoped they would get it.

NEIL WALKER

Chapter Forty-Five

As they walked through the main doors, they entered the majestic hallway with its polished wooden floors. The chandelier hanging from the extremely high ceiling was illuminating the place, as they made their way inside.

John tapped Ali on the shoulder as they approached the carpeted staircase, pointed at him and pointed upwards. He then pointed at himself, before pointing straight ahead. This was to signal that Ali should proceed up the stairs and check the upstairs of the house, while John would search downstairs.

Ali nodded his understanding and agreement and set off up the carpeted staircase.

John turned his attention and focus to the space right in front of him, as he made his way through the hallway, his gun at the ready to open fire at the first sign of life.

He entered the main hall, to hear music blaring through the sound system. It was the track 'Belter' by Powderfinger. This was possibly some kind of sick joke on the part of his enemies, as John was a well-known fan and enthusiast of the band.

The TV was on, with the demo of a soccer game playing loudly on it through the attached PlayStation 2. This situation quickly appeared to John to have been set up for his benefit - a room full of noisy and colourful distractions for him.

He scanned the room with his eyes, his head on a swivel. Failure to notice something could cost him his life. His gun was ready to fire in his outstretched right hand, his left hand still carrying the bag of weapons.

The main hall was a huge room with a wooden balcony running right round above it, matching the flooring and wood panelled walls. There was a lot for his eyes to examine, as he prepared to be attacked.

There were the black leather sofas in front of the TV that could shield an attacker, as well as other furniture scattered around the hall.

There were the La-Z-Boy reclining chairs at the end of the hall John had entered through, by the stereo and pool tables. John had already scanned those for signs of life, however, and was almost positive they were clear.

He didn't have to wonder where the attack would come from for much longer, as a gunshot whistled past his head. The bullet hit the wood panelled pillar beside him and he dropped to the ground for cover.

Another shot rang out, as he scrambled for the cover of one of the pool tables, at the same time looking upwards across the hall, in the direction where the gunfire was coming from.

He saw Peter firing a pistol from high up in the balcony area to his right, from behind one of the wood panelled pillars.

John made it to the relative safety of the pool table, as another bullet impacted right on the edge of it, just above where his head was as he crouched behind it. He paid no attention to this, as he opened up his weapons bag on the floor and began quickly pulling out the additional .45 automatics from within it.

Occasional bullets continued to strike the pool table, in the area right above his head, as John prepared to take action.

He took two of the .45s from his weapons bag and tucked them into the front of his trousers. He then took another one out and tucked it into the back of his trousers.

Leaving one in the bag, he took another one out and took hold of it in his left hand, sticking with the .45 he had been wielding since he entered Nathan House in his right.

He took a few quick breaths, psyching himself up to return fire. Immediately after the next incoming bullet impacted on the pool table, he sprang up to his feet and opened fire with the two .45s in his hands.

Peter sought shelter behind the wood panelled pillar he had been using for cover and disappeared from view. John did not stop firing though, aiming for and hitting the sides of the pillar at either side of where Peter's head was hiding.

He fired relentlessly until both .45s were out of bullets, before dropping both pistols to the ground like hot bricks.

Peter peaked his head round from behind the pillar, but before he could start firing again, John pulled out the two .45s that had been tucked into the front of his trousers and opened fire with them.

This sent Peter back into hiding behind the pillar, squirming as the bullets impacted in tandem at either side of his head, splintering the wood so that it was erupting in a flurry of shards around his face.

As soon as the gunfire ceased, John dropped the two empty pistols from his hands and Peter spun out from behind the pillar to take his shot.

As Peter raised his gun to fire again, John pulled out the .45 that was tucked into the back of his trousers.

Peter pulled the trigger on his pistol a split second before John could fire his, but rushed his shot. The bullet flew past the right side of John's head, hitting the wall behind him.

John made no such mistake with his shot, however, hitting Peter in the face. The bullet struck Peter's head with devastating effect, going clean through and exploding with a huge, bloody exit wound out of the back of it.

John had literally blown his brains out.

As Peter's lifeless body slumped backwards and to the right, it toppled over the balcony and landed in a bloody mess on the wooden floor of the main hall.

John did not need to check that he was dead; he knew that he had killed him with a precision piece of shooting.

He had killed a man who he had believed to be his good and trusted friend only a matter of hours previously. He felt no sense of guilt though, only a sense of purpose.

Peter was dead, but Kate and Simon were still alive. This he would have to change.

NEIL WALKER

Chapter Forty-Six

Ali was unfamiliar with his surroundings, as he carefully and systematically made his way around the upstairs of this huge, magnificent mansion house.

He had heard the gunfire coming from downstairs, but remained focused on his task at hand. He reasoned that John could take of himself, and that he probably had.

He heard noise coming from within the next room in his search, and grasped the door handle tight with his left hand, ready to open it quickly and charge through. He had his pistol ready to fire in his other hand.

As he crashed through the door and aimed his gun, he found himself in the screening room: a scaled down cinema. This was not what he was expecting.

Coming out of the quietly ticking projector on to the small cinema screen was the noisy finale of the film Scarface. This is what Ali had heard from outside and now that he was inside the room it was a lot louder.

The movie in the projector had not been changed since the screening room had last been used on Boxing Day. On this occasion, however, it had been switched on for the purpose of visual and audio distraction, rather than cinematic viewing pleasure.

Ali tried hard not to be distracted by Tony Montana's cocaine-fuelled ranting and shooting. He needed to concentrate on real life and his own imminent gunfight.

Before he could get a shot off, Kate popped up from behind the front row of cinema seats and fired on him with a pump action shotgun.

She hit him in the chest, before leaping up on to the backrests of the row of seats she been hiding behind. She then jumped forwards from one backrest to the other, until she reached the back of the screening room, rushing out the door as Ali slumped back against the wall.

Ali had been hit, but the bulletproof vest had taken the impact. It still hurt him a lot and winded him, but he was alive and okay to continue.

He quickly gathered himself and ran out of the screening room in pursuit of Kate.

Ali scanned the hallways, doors and stairs for signs of movement or clues as to where Kate was hiding. He now felt sure she was still upstairs, as she would not have had time to make it down the staircase before he had emerged back through the door of the screening room.

It didn't take long before he noticed a door ajar that he was almost positive had been closed before. He hadn't searched this room yet and gingerly made his way into the doorway.

He was entering a large bedroom and could see the foot of the bed at the far side of the room as he entered. Holding his gun in a standard two-hand grip in front of him, he made his way very slowly through the doorway. He had the trigger partly squeezed already, as he felt almost certain that she was in there.

As his gun entered the room - just passing the edge of the open door - the door slammed on him from the right side with a huge amount of force.

Kate had kicked it on him as powerfully as she could and as it hit his forearms, his gun went off, firing a single shot into the far wall.

Kate slammed the butt of her shogun down on his wrists, forcing him to drop his pistol. She then swung upwards with the butt of the shotgun, with a view to cracking Ali in the face with it.

Ali reacted quickly and ducked his head to the left, avoiding the impending blow. He then caught her on the right side of her face with a powerful left hook, sending her stumbling back the way she had come.

Ali swiftly picked up his gun from the ground, in a single bobbing motion, as Kate regained her footing and composure and aimed her pump action shotgun at him.

He managed to pick up his pistol and duck back out through the door, before the gunfire from the shotgun impacted with ferocity on the bedroom wall. Kate then pumped the shotgun and fired again, this time angling her shot with the hope of catching Ali as he stood back in the hallway.

The shot missed and Ali immediately opened fire with his automatic pistol, before she could get another shot off.

His pistol was a fully loaded Beretta 9mm, so he had a lot of rounds to shoot and he planned to use them liberally - fifteen in the clip and one in the pipe, minus the one bullet from the accidental discharge when Kate had hit him with the door.

He fired the first six shots in rapid succession, as he advanced back through the doorway. He then fired five more shots around the door, until he heard a scream and the smash of glass from within.

He got into the room just in time to see the last flash of Kate flying through the upstairs window, backwards into the dark night, the blood spray still in the air from where his bullet had hit her.

He slumped back against the wall and slid down it, hurt and physically drained, but relieved.

As he caught his breath, Ali spoke to himself.

"Thank fuck for that. What a fucking bitch."

He took a few moments to compose himself and get his breath back, before he would have to finish his search of the upstairs and see who was left to kill.

Chapter Forty-Seven

John had reloaded all five of the .45 automatics he had used so far, plus he still had the sixth one lying unused in the weapons-filled sports bag he was carrying.

As he entered the large gym area of the house, he had two .45s tucked into the front of his trousers and a further two tucked into the back of his trousers.

While one of them still remained in the weapons bag that he was once again carrying in his left hand, he was holding the other .45 automatic in the hand of his outstretched right arm. He was ready to fire with split second timing and his usual accuracy, as soon as a target presented itself.

As he made his way into the gym, scanning for human targets, it wasn't long before he had something to fire at.

A flash of movement in one of the mirrors that made up the mirrored wall at the side of the gym caught his eye. It was a reflection of Simon popping up from behind the base of the boxing ring; gun in hand, ready to fire on him.

John was too quick for him though, as he spun to face the boxing ring.

He aimed and fired his pistol, before Simon could get his shot off. The bullet hit Simon's right hand - going right through it - causing him to scream out in pain and drop his gun.

John dropped his weapons bag and ran across the room to the boxing ring, gun at the ready.

He got to the boxing ring to find Simon cowering behind it, his gun lying a few feet away from him on the floor. He was holding his bloody right hand with his left, trying to comfort himself.

John stood over him, aiming the .45 down at his head.

"Get up!" he shouted at him.

Simon paused for a second, before struggling to his feet as instructed.

As soon as Simon was standing up, John uncocked the hammer on the .45 he was holding and pulled out a second .45 from the back of his trousers.

He then skilfully threw them up a couple of inches in the air, in such a way that they spun around and he was able to catch both of them by the barrels. He began fiercely pistol-whipping Simon with the handles of both .45s at once, each one battering either side of his head and upper body.

Simon tried to protect himself with his arms, but it was no good, as John energetically beat him with the heavy pistols, in a quick succession of blows from a variety of angles.

Simon was once again screaming in pain, as the sharp and heavy metallic blows rained down on him. He fell back against the base of the boxing ring and started to lose consciousness.

At this point, John stopped battering him. He tucked one of the bloodied pistols into its original position in the back of his trousers and used his now free left hand to sharply slap Simon in the face, stinging him back into full consciousness.

"Stay with me Simon! I'm not finished with you yet."

John kicked Simon's gun across the gym away from him and dashed across the room to grab the weapons bag, getting back to Simon as quickly as he could. Simon hadn't moved; he was conscious, but too badly hurt to jump to his feet or try to do anything.

John then put the blood-soaked .45 from his right hand into the weapons bag and pulled out a choker style dog leash. He held it up to Simon's face.

"Remember this?"

Without waiting for an answer, he slipped the collar of the choke lead around Simon's neck and pulled the leash tight.

He then began trailing a gasping Simon across the floor of the gym, on his hands and knees behind him, with the leash in his right hand. He was once again carrying the weapons bag in his left.

John dragged him all the way through the house on his hands and knees, as Simon struggled to breathe and had no choice but to scurry behind him, trying to use brief moments of relief in the choking to catch his breath.

They got to the bottom of the main staircase just as Ali was at the top of it, about to walk down the stairs.

"Stay there mate, we're coming up!" John shouted up to him.

Ali stayed put, while John forcefully dragged a drooling, wheezing Simon up the carpeted staircase, as he bled all over it from his freshly wounded hand and the deep cuts on his head.

Once they were at the top of the stairs, John led Ali, and trailed Simon, to the main office. John knew Simon would have taken this office - which had been Doug's during his time in The Brotherhood - as his personal headquarters.

He dragged him across the floor and around behind the large wooden desk. He then swung the wooden door on the right hand side of it open, to reveal the poorly concealed in-built safe, which was the same one Doug had used.

John removed the dog collar and Simon lay there gasping for breath, while John put the weapons bag down on top of the large wooden desk and took a couple of seconds to compose himself.

As he turned to face him, with Ali at his side, Simon got his breath back enough to speak.

"Don't kill me mate. Please don't fucking kill me."

Ali and John both laughed at this in tandem. It was funny to see this notoriously merciless gang leader now down on the ground, pathetically begging for mercy.

"And why the fuck would I let you live?" John asked him.

"I'll give you everything. The safe is full to capacity with money and drugs, probably way more than you took the last time. I'll give it to you without a struggle if you let me live. What do you have to gain by killing me?"

John couldn't believe the audacity of what he was hearing.

"I'd gain the satisfaction of watching you die in front of me."

"Come on Johnny Boy, let me live and I'll make you a millionaire. Plus you'll never hear from me again."

Less than a year ago, John had been in this office, standing over Doug in a similar situation. He had been surprised at how quickly Doug gave up the combination to the very same safe under torture, but now here was Simon offering to just tell it to him outright to save his own life.

"Simon, do you really think after everything you've done, all the hurt you've caused, you deserve to live; to get away with it?"

"Johnny Boy, you'll be set up for life. All you've got to do is let me live."

"Up to you John," chipped in Ali.

He was growing weary of Simon's pleading, but liked the sound of the contents of the safe.

"You can't let him kill me either John. I know you're generally a man of your word and if you promise that neither of you will kill me, you two can take everything in the safe and split it."

Ali hadn't been wronged directly by Simon in the same way that John had and looked to him to make the call. John paused for what seemed to Simon like an eternity, as he weighed up his options.

Just as the tension in the room reached an almost unbearable level, John broke the silence.

"Okay, fuck it. You're right; I've got nothing to gain by killing you. Getting the contents of the safe is worth leaving you alive. Lisa never has to know and me and Ali can split the proceeds."

Simon sighed with relief, before wanting to once again clarify the terms and conditions of their arrangement.

"So, I tell you the combination to the safe and you promise me - on the lives of your mother and your girlfriend - that neither you or Ali will kill me."

"I promise."

"No offence John, but I'm going to need to hear it; the full thing."

John smiled, well aware of why Simon was being so cautious. The combination to the safe was the only bargaining chip he had left and he wasn't going to give it up unless he was sure it was going to save his life.

"I John Kennedy, promise you Simon Pollack, leader of The Brotherhood, that if you give up the combination to that safe, then neither me or Ali will kill you. I swear it on the lives of my mother and my girlfriend."

Simon was now satisfied and Ali was happy enough with the outcome, if a little surprised. He was looking forward to his cut of whatever was in the safe and felt it was up to John, under the circumstances, to decide if Simon lived or died.

"You want to do the honours mate?" John said to Ali, gesturing towards the safe.

Ali nodded and knelt down in front of the safe, before looking to Simon for the combination. Simon duly obliged and safe was soon open, revealing a huge pile of money and drugs.

"Holy shit!" Ali exclaimed, as he stood up and stepped back to take in the sight of this huge haul.

"Fucking hell mate, we're rich," he said, turning to John.

Chapter Forty-Eight

John looked on emotionless at the sight before him. There were a ridiculous amount of money bundles and drug bags, packed tightly in the now open safe. Simon was sitting upright on the ground beside it.

Simon seemed to be more relieved and happy about saving his life, than he seemed annoyed about losing his personal treasure stash.

"Enjoy it lads. Like I said, you'll never have to worry about me again," Simon announced to the pair.

John didn't respond to him, simply turning to the large wooden desk and reaching both hands into his weapons bag. He then pulled out the two .45 automatic pistols from within it - one covered in Simon's blood, the other so far unused.

He turned to face Simon, aiming the two .45s at him, with both arms outstretched, pointed in his direction.

"What the fuck John? You got what you wanted! You promised not to kill me! You swore on your mother's life! You swore on Lisa's life!"

"Don't you ever say her name," were John's only words.

He opened fire with both guns at once, firing them in tandem.

Ali was shocked by this turn of events and covered his ears to block out the loud gunshots, echoing through the wood panelled room.

John emptied both guns into Simon's legs, as he yelled out in agony.

His howls had been largely drowned out by the gunfire from the two weapons, but they were now very much audible, as John dropped the two empty .45s on the floor in front of him.

He then quickly pulled out the two .45s that he had tucked into the front of his trousers and opened fire with them in the same way, firing them in tandem into Simon's legs. The gunfire once again drowned out the anguished cries from Simon.

John emptied these guns into Simon's legs as well, before dropping them beside the first two empty pistols on the floor in front of him.

Without any delay, he pulled out the remaining two .45s that had been tucked into the back of his trousers and opened fire on Simon again, firing both weapons simultaneously as he had before.

This time he fired on both of Simon's arms, turning them into the same shredded, bloody messes that he had made of his legs.

Once these two pistols ran out of bullets, he calmly stepped over to the wooden desk and placed them into his weapons bag.

He then turned back and picked up the four empty guns he had dropped on the floor, returning to the desk and placing them into the weapons bag as well. Turning around to face an agonised and screaming Simon, he stepped towards him and knelt down in front of him.

"You're bleeding a lot mate, in case you haven't noticed. I haven't killed you though buddy. On the off chance you can survive these wounds, I've just got one thing to say to you."

Simon was too busy shrieking to respond in any way, before John delivered his final words to him.

"Live with this."

Simon continued wailing and moaning, as John and Ali went down and got the extra sports bags from the boot of the car, putting the weapons bag back into the boot.

They took off their bulletproof vests while they were down there, throwing them into the boot as well, before making their way back up to the office and emptying the contents of the safe into the extra sports bags.

As they left the office, Simon was still alive; John had kept his promise, although not in the way that Simon had hoped.

They made their way down the main staircase with their bags of drugs and money, and were on their way out through the main doors, when they heard the hammer of a pistol cock behind them.

A voice that was familiar to John then spoke to them.

"Drop the bags and turn around."

John recognised the voice straight away; it was Stuart. John had been so carried away with finally getting his hands on Simon, that he hadn't fully completed his search of the downstairs of the house and had missed his old friend, who had been hiding on the shooting range.

Stuart now had the drop on them.

Both John and Ali dropped their bags and turned to face Stuart, with their hands in the air.

Chapter Forty-Nine

When John was in The Brotherhood, Stuart had been his best friend in the gang. Even Michael, the guy he had travelled round the world with and who had got him into the gang in the first place, hadn't been as close a friend to him as Stuart had been during those eight months of his life.

By the end of his time in the gang, The Brotherhood had murdered Michael and he had felt nothing but contempt for his fellow gang members - his 'brothers' - with the exception of Stuart.

The majority of the guilt he had felt about the way he left The Brotherhood was about the position he had left Stuart in.

He didn't know if Stuart understood why he had done what he had done. He wasn't sure if he had been angered by it, or if he resented John for not trusting him enough to involve him in his plan.

Now he would find out, however, as Stuart had a gun pointed at him and held his life - and the life of Ali - in his hands.

"Hello Stuart," he said, greeting him cautiously.

"Hello John, it's been a while," Stuart replied, reciprocating John's tone.

"Sorry about the way I left things mate."

"Why did you do it man?" Stuart asked him.

He already believed he knew the answer.

John knew this was not a time to beat around the bush or hold back about his thoughts and feelings. If he was going to be killed in this moment - based on what he said - then he was going to tell the absolute truth and lay all his cards on the table.

If Stuart heard his explanation and chose to go ahead and kill him anyway, then so be it.

"Michael. I couldn't get past what happened to him and to his mother. I know I played a part in it at the time, but I couldn't live with it afterwards. The only thing I could think to do was kill Doug and Sanjay when I had the chance and take down the gang."

"Well you did the first bit, but all that killing those two did was hand the gang over to an even sicker cunt."

"I know mate. I suppose I didn't realise how much Simon knew and how tied in he was to Doug and Sanjay and the way the gang operated from the top down. If I had known that, I'd never have done things the way I did. Do you know what he did to me and my girlfriend in Sydney?"

"I only heard about it afterwards. I'm sorry John. Simon is a disgusting excuse for a human being."

"He always was."

"Yeah; I think I even warned you about Simon on your first night here."

"You did. You could not have been more right about him."

"It's not that easy to leave The Brotherhood; you know that. I'm just glad it's all over now," said Stuart.

"Thank fuck," agreed John.

"I still think about Michael and his mum too you know."

"I know you do."

Stuart uncocked the hammer of the pistol he was holding and lowered it down by his side.

"Good luck mate," Stuart said to John, smiling.

"Good luck," John replied, smiling back.

He and Ali turned around to walk through the doors, but John knelt down, before he started walking, and unzipped one of the recently filled sports bags.

Stuart was looking on warily and was ready to raise his pistol again, if John was tricking him.

John stood up with two large bundles of fifty pound notes in each hand, turned back and threw them to Stuart. They landed at his feet and he relaxed, once again smiling at John.

"Don't spend all that in the one shop," John joked.

He turned, kneeled down, zipped up the bag again and picked it up.

John and Ali walked out through the doors and carried the sports bags to the car, putting them in the boot, on top of the bulletproof vests and beside the weapons bag.

John slammed the car boot shut and he and Ali got quickly into the car, exchanging no words about what had just transpired inside the house.

As they began driving out of the magnificent grounds of Nathan House, John stared out at them through the darkness, taking a last look. He drove away hoping never to set eyes on the place again.

Chapter Fifty

As John sat in the departure lounge of Belfast International Airport, he carefully watched each person walk in as they arrived.

He had made sure that Lisa had got the tickets he bought for her and she still had time to get there before last call for their flights. He had booked them on connecting flights, flying to Sydney via London and Hong Kong.

While she still had a little time to get there and catch their first flight, there was not much time to spare. If she was planning to go with him, she was cutting it very fine indeed.

He didn't know if she was going to come. The last time he'd spoken with her, she didn't know what she was going to do.

He'd been in Belfast for almost six weeks after he'd got back from Manchester and had seen her every chance he got. She still hadn't seemed entirely herself, after what had happened four months before.

This was, of course, understandable, although John could tell she was improving, day on day, week on week.

Ali and his gang had been really helpful after the events of New Year's Eve and had made sure that he and Blair had somewhere to stay in Manchester and had everything they needed, including off the books medical care.

They had parted on good terms and split the money and drugs down the middle. John even threw in the guns and bulletproof vests for Ali as a bonus.

They had both got what they wanted out of their alliance and Ali was firmly in place to be the new king of the Manchester underworld.

Ali and his gang had cleaned up everything too, so there was no heat to run from in terms of the law. There would be a lot of missing persons as time went on, but no evidence of what had happened and no trail leading to them.

Once Blair had been well enough and the pair had looked good enough to travel to Belfast without drawing stares, they had got the boat back from Liverpool.

Blair had stayed with him at his mother's house, while he recovered from what John told his mother was a bad car accident. He had been well fed and looked after, and the pair had had a chance to unwind and get their strength and fitness back.

Blair would be fine, although his face would never be quite as pretty as it had been before.

They had made arrangements to get the money and drugs into Australia and past customs, which they managed to do without problems. Blair then followed the money and drugs to Sydney shortly afterwards.

Luckily, they still had loyal guys working for them in Sydney, to help them pull off this transfer of assets and guard the money and drugs until Blair got back. Obviously, these guys would get their cut, as well as being kept in the game with this new stock of chemical supplies.

John would meet up with Blair once he got to Sydney and make sure everything was running smoothly, before taking his cut of the money and leaving the drug business behind forever.

He planned to take his share of the money and head off to make a fresh start, hopefully with Lisa by his side.

He had been waiting in the airport for a long time, having made a point of getting there early, to make sure Lisa didn't arrive before he got there. He couldn't risk her thinking he had stood her up or wasn't coming.

John wanted to embark on a new life with her more than anything.

The time spent staring at the unfamiliar faces, as they streamed into the airport, also gave him plenty of time to reflect.

He had realised that it was exactly a year to the day since he'd been lying on his back on the grass in the grounds of Nathan House, trying to forget himself.

He had come a long way since then and been through a lifetime's worth of angst and turmoil. Now he hoped all that would very soon be behind him.

While he was in Belfast, he had considered contacting Alan's mother, or one of his siblings. He knew them all well and he felt for them.

He absolutely hated the thought of the torment they would feel, once they realised he was missing. Ultimately, he had decided that knowing the true horror of the details of what had happened to Alan would be far more devastating than just being unable to find him.

Maybe he would change his mind in time and put them out of their misery, into potentially worse misery. For now, he had to focus on himself, his plan to make a fresh start, and his hopes for him and Lisa.

As the last call for their first flight - the flight to London - rang out over the public address system, he realised he would have to give up on the Lisa relationship for now.

He wasn't completely surprised that she hadn't come. After all, look at how he'd lied to her and look at what had happened to her because of him.

John stood up from the metal seat he had been sitting on and turned around to gather up his hand luggage bag and the items he'd bought in the airport shop. As he did so, he felt a tap on the shoulder.

He spun round to see a grinning Lisa standing behind him.

The pair of them then just stood there, looking at each other and smiling. John was overwhelmed with emotion and was lost for words.

It was left up to Lisa to break the silence.

"Let's go."

THE END

NEIL WALKER

I hope you have enjoyed this novel. Please take a moment to leave a review on Amazon.

Reviews are a critical factor in the success of any novel and are a powerful buying tool to help readers find the right book. As an author, I really appreciate it when readers review my work and I very much enjoy reading their thoughts.

To leave a review, just go to the Amazon page for Drug Gang Vengeance and then click on 'write a customer review'.

And if you want to see how the Drug Gang story concludes, the details of the third and final book in the series are over the page.

Many thanks,

Neil Walker

NEIL WALKER

PART THREE OF THE DRUG GANG TRILOGY AVAILABLE NOW!

Drug Gang Takedown: Drug Gang Part III by Neil Walker

ALL BAD THINGS MUST COME TO AN END…

THIS TIME IT'S WAR!

Drug Gang Takedown is the third crime thriller in the bestselling Drug Gang series.

Former drug dealer John Kennedy returns to Sydney to collect the money he is owed, to start a new life. Despite his best efforts to leave the drug world in the past, he quickly finds himself caught in the middle of the biggest drug war in Australian history…

FINAL PART OF THE DRUG GANG TRILOGY.

NEIL WALKER

ABOUT THE AUTHOR

Neil Walker is the bestselling Belfast author of hard-hitting crime fiction. His works include the acclaimed crime thriller Drug Gang and its sequel Drug Gang Vengeance.

Both of these controversial bestsellers are part of the Drug Gang Trilogy and are set in the drug dealing underworld of Manchester, Sydney and Belfast in the early 2000s.

The third and final Drug Gang novel, Drug Gang Takedown, was published in January 2019 and quickly became a bestseller.

To learn more, visit the author's social media pages:

twitter.com/neilwalkerwrote

facebook.com/neilwalkerauthor

instagram.com/neilwalkerauthor

#DrugGang
#DrugGangVengeance
#DrugGangTakedown
#DrugGangTrilogy

Printed in Great Britain
by Amazon